Under My Window

To J...

Nov. 16/2021

Under My Window

A Compilation of Short Stories

Navid Sorkhou

UNDER MY WINDOW
A COMPILATION OF SHORT STORIES

Copyright © 2015 Navid Sorkhou.

All rights reserved. No part of this book may be used or reproduced by any means, graphic, electronic, or mechanical, including photocopying, recording, taping or by any information storage retrieval system without the written permission of the publisher except in the case of brief quotations embodied in critical articles and reviews.

This is a work of fiction. All of the characters, names, incidents, organizations, and dialogue in this novel are either the products of the author's imagination or are used fictitiously.

iUniverse books may be ordered through booksellers or by contacting:

iUniverse
1663 Liberty Drive
Bloomington, IN 47403
www.iuniverse.com
1-800-Authors (1-800-288-4677)

Because of the dynamic nature of the Internet, any web addresses or links contained in this book may have changed since publication and may no longer be valid. The views expressed in this work are solely those of the author and do not necessarily reflect the views of the publisher, and the publisher hereby disclaims any responsibility for them.

Any people depicted in stock imagery provided by Thinkstock are models, and such images are being used for illustrative purposes only.
Certain stock imagery © Thinkstock.

ISBN: 978-1-4917-6115-1 (sc)
ISBN: 978-1-4917-6124-3 (hc)
ISBN: 978-1-4917-6116-8 (e)

Library of Congress Control Number: 2015902781

Print information available on the last page.

iUniverse rev. date: 02/18/2015

Under My Window is a compilation of fictional stories that I came up with by listening to the sounds outside my bedroom window on Taylor Street in Vancouver. I moved to the neighborhood in February 2006 and lived there until June 2009. I can proudly say I lived at one of the most unique addresses in Vancouver, a great place to start off *Under My Window*.

The sounds! Trying to sleep early at Taylor was not so easy. With the window open and the fine early summer breeze caressing the room, the different street sounds could not be ignored. There is no escaping the sounds from the street mixed up with the sounds in your own head. Hence, the book title Under *My Window*.

I won't reveal too much here about the story lines, the characters, and the "why that"? In this book the story lines could be real, and the characters fictional, or vice versa. As for the "why that?" you can be the judge: you decide for yourself why I chose that story and those characters. I would love to hear your thoughts. Also, throughout the story I have asked for your input. I hope to hear back from you.

So enjoy the book, and after reading it I hope your mind and heart are more open and you will promise yourself to strive to become better and better. Change is only possible with an open mind. With Change one can always become better and better and better. Best is difficult to achieve but still very much attainable. And, perfection is impossible.

Thank you.

I wrote this book listening to the following artists' music:

Pink Floyd, Tupac, Bob Marley, Adele, DJ Siavash Ashrafiani, Tiesto, Lynyrd Skynard, Al Green, U2, Coldplay, DJ Eric Allen, Mumford & Sons, Led Zeppelin, Radiohead, Dire Straits, The Doors, Marvin Gaye, Vivaldi, Lumineers, Mozart, Luciano Pavarotti, Kanye West, Michael Jackson, Mother Mother, DJ Eric Lewis, Rod Stewart, Tragically Hip, Colin James, John Lee Hooker, Eagles, Fleetwood Mac, Supertramp, Simply Red, Hannah Georges, Kings of Leon, DJ Chelsea Joelle.

Story 1

Sammy and Luci

It is time to go to bed. What happened to her? She suddenly stopped all communication with me. I hope that she is fine and getting better. I cannot get it out of my head. Come on; I am sure I was not much help with her situation. I wish I could make it up to her, but why do something unpleasant in the first place that you feel the need to make up for?

The window is open. It is early summer, and it is nice out. The air is cooler than the last few days, but it feels lovely. It is such a pleasant change from the short heat wave.

A man is talking very fast outside, just talking, and he is walking back and forth. He is mumbling, and all of a sudden his voice grows very loud.

"I think everyone is looking at me. Why is everyone looking at me? I am not doing anything. Did I ask for money or anything? No. Then why are they looking at me?" I look down and see that there is no one else in the street at that moment. He is by himself.

Sammy, a tall Caucasian man of about 130 pounds, is an addict. He is addicted to crack cocaine and meth. This deep into drugs, he has written his own death sentence; sooner than later he is dead if serious help is not found.

Sammy was a car salesman. A successful salesman, to boot, was selling high end new cars. He had a nice family and a nice picket-fence house. He was rolling in the dough. I am talking about two years in a row of over 200 G's per year. Enough money to make many of their dreams come true. Since he was a control freak, he controlled the money. The wife had no say in the running of the finances. Actually, she had not much say in about anything. She would get a good chunk of allowance every month for running the home. Sammy also gave her money for her personal expenses. He did not spare any money when it came to his wife and children. He made sure they were provided for. He had everything but he still felt empty. He felt something was missing in his life.

Selling cars is fast-paced, shrewd, and thrilling. He was lacking that in his home life, and more than anything he wanted a thrill in his personal life. He had the money for it, but he did not know what kind of a thrill would be exciting to him. He was getting bored with his home life. He felt he was not being challenged there anymore. He provided and worked diligently to achieve a good home for his family, but now, when he got into his car to head home, it was not like before. Before, he looked forward to going home. He couldn't wait. He had ants in his pants all day just waiting to go home. He showed customers pictures of his wife and children whenever he got the chance. He glowed with the love he had for his family, and his customers picked up on that. His success was because of his family.

But now that happiness and giddiness was not there anymore when he turned the ignition key to head home. He was not happy when he got into his expensive, fully loaded, fast and comfortable car, with its stereo system with built-in equalizer and eight strategically placed speakers! Sammy loves music. He even likes country and western. Not all types of country and western, like the really heavy, twangy, sad country music. Not his style. But he really likes Johnny Cash, Willie Nelson, Dwight Yoakam, Shania Twain, Tim McGraw, and the Dixie Chicks. Sammy lived his life crassly through Johnny and Willie and he respected the Dixie Chicks cause they had balls! He also liked the country songs by the Eagles and one of his all time favorite bands, Lynyrd Skynard. And Elvis! Sammy is listening to new Eminem today and singing along with him. The words he knows.

Sammy really does not have anyone to restrict him. As a child he got away with murder. Sammy's wife (since this is about Sammy and Luci, and Luci is not Sammy's wife, you give Sammy's wife any name you see fit) was doing her own thing. As long as the money was coming in and she was taking care of herself and her children, she did not care what was happening with Sammy or to Sammy. She loved Sammy but loved her kids more. She wanted all the comforts for her daughters and she did everything with them. She would take them shopping, to restaurants, visiting with friends, and on trips. That is how she made herself happy, being with her kids. If Sammy came along, fine; but if he didn't, she would take the kids and kiss Sammy on the lips and leave him at home all by himself. She thought Sammy was happy like this. He had his good job, a faithful wife totally dedicated to their children, and beautiful daughters who loved their daddy. But did they really love Dad or just what Dad was providing for them? Would they still love Dad if he had no money to provide for them or a nice home for them to live in?

Sammy really did not enjoy staying at home all by himself. He easily got bored just hanging around the house in his lonesome. Where is my family? Why am I not with them? They asked me to come, but I only will be in their way. Let them do their own thing. I'll go with them next time. Next time comes, and again the excuse that I am tired and need to rest. Sammy's wife would not, even once, insist on him coming with them. Maybe that was all he was looking for: Please, honey come with us; we want you to come with us; we are not going if you don't come. He got none of that. Instead he would get, "Oh, okay. Me and the kids are going to a movie, then to eat out with their friends. Have a good night, honey." Kiss on the lips and out the door.

Sammy then decided that he needed some excitement in his life away from his work and home. He decided he was going to hang out with the guys at work more often instead of going to a home that eventually would be empty during the night. Sammy's wife went out pretty much every night with their girls (reader: you can also name the daughters). On the rare occasions that they were home, she would make sure the kids were busy with something, so really no quality time was spent with Dad. The girls didn't mind this arrangement either. Their perception of their dad was not much of love but more of duty.

He didn't have any real buddies. He had maybe four friends he had known since high school. Like him, his high school chums were married with children. Three out of four did hardly anything outside their family activities. But they did really cool stuff. One of Sammy's friends took his family on a hot air balloon camping trip the year before. They had so much fun. They came over and showed the pictures to Sammy and his family. The other guys would visit during Christmas and birthdays and usually talk about the old times. Not about what is happening right now in their lives. Mostly the women talked about that, their lives today. But the guys mostly talked about the good old high school and college days. Sammy did not go to college, and he was always embarrassed about it in front of his close friends.

The guys at work were more like him. Some had wives; majority of them were divorced, with little or no higher education. So he could relate to them better than the other group of friends. The guys at work were also fun. So he started hanging out with the work buddies and checking out the local strip bars. The guys at work had been on Sammy's case to come out with them and have a good time. *Why can't I do that?* Sammy would ask himself. *There is no reason that says I can't do that. I am going to do it.* After awhile night clubs and casinos were added to the roster. When you are buying drinks for every Tanya, Doris, and Sherry and gambling at the same time, you can go through a lot of cash faster than you can say fun times. He liked it, though. Way too much. Chicks everywhere and they gave more attention to him than anyone he knew, certainly more than his wife and kids. Sammy was now getting attention from a bunch of strangers who made him feel good about himself.

Then came the drugs. Let's make it more fun and exciting and kinky and out of this world and, and, and ... let's just *fly*! How high do you think you can get? *Really High! I want to be so high that I want to feel like I am strapped to a rocket being shot up toward the moon at 900 miles an hour. I want to be so high so can I feel like that.*

"I love to get fucked when I am high on coke and G. I get so horny when I am on G. This is the time Sammy befriended Luci. Luscious Luci. "Please, Sammy, get me some coke, and I will do anything you want me to. I will love you forever, baby. Please believe me baby, Sammy, I love you baby," Luci tells Sammy.

He started spending ridiculous amounts of money on women, booze and drugs. Meanwhile, he remained responsible for providing for his family. "Oh my God. I cannot cope with this. This is too much for me to handle. My wife hates me, and my children are scared of me. I need some meth right now. Yeah, that is what I need. I need to cope with this problem. I better get hold of Luci." Sammy's drug problem was getting worse and worse each day. He needed drugs to cope with his everyday life now.

Telephone ring, ring, ring. "Come on, Luci, pick up please, Luci pick up, pleeeeease."

"Hello." Luci's voice hoarse and scratchy, that dry cough sound. The "h" sounds like a deep spit building up in the throat and wanting to jump out. She coughs.

"It's me. Sammy. I need to see you. I need to get something from you."
"You have money, Sammy?"

"Yes, I do. When can I see you and where? Please soon. Please. I am going through some hard times right now, and I need to think. I need the stuff to help me think."

"Don't worry, Sammy. I got what you need, baby. I can be at the corner in front of 7-Eleven in minutes. Bring $40 for now, and I'll fix you up. Don't worry, baby. Everything is going to be all right. Have I ever lied to you, baby? I am the only honest person in your life, baby."

"Oh, you are the best, Luci. But I only have $30 baby. Please. That is all I have, baby."

"I said $40. Find the other ten and then call me. I am not going to waste my time for thirty bucks, *baby*. Find the other ten and then call me. I'm waiting for your call."

"You know how long it is going to take me to gather ten bucks, Luci? Please, Luci, I will make it up to you. I really need it right now. Luci, you know I'm good for it. Please, Luci. Please." Sammy breaks down on the phone and starts crying hard and loud, his emotions coming out in his cry all at once. He is bashing the telephone headset into his head, and it hurts. He is feeling the sharp pain inside his temple. A throbbing pain like someone took a knife and cut into his brain. All he wants right now is to either have the hit or die.

"Okay, okay. Don't fucking freak out on me, Sammy. Bring me what you have. Along the way, if you can steal anything, anything worthy, no fucking junk, it is mine. Try to bring forty bucks. See you in ten minutes."

Still crying. "thank you, Luci. Thank you."

Luci had a strange childhood. She was conceived from a night of lust, and therefore for all the wrong reasons. Luci's mom (again the same here, my dear reader: you give her a name and even a character) was bored with her life. Her beauty attracted many men, but still, men's divine attention to her bored her even more. She wanted a challenge, and what better challenge than being a mother? There you go: *I want to be a mom.* So, Luci's mom got pregnant with Luci, but having Luci did not really stop her from her party life. No! She still wanted to have her fun. She still went to bars and tried hard to not smoke and drink but did not try hard enough. When she was four months into her pregnancy, she got so sick from drinking and puked so violently that she stopped drinking for the rest of her pregnancy, but her smoking didn't stop.

Finally, Luci was born, after nine months and three days. A beautiful healthy girl with emerald eyes and golden hair! Her hair was so fine it was the softest thing Luci's mom had ever touched in her life. Luci was cared for properly until she got to be six months old. That is when Luci's mom decided enough was enough, that it was time to go out and have some fun.

Luci was now her new doll. A beautiful, smiling, bright-eyed live doll. At six months old, she wouldn't know what was going on. Luci's mother thought, *I'll just get a nice big purse and put her in there and go to my favorite watering hole and have a drink or two and just chit-chat and then come home. I'll just do this once a week. That is reasonable. I wouldn't want to leave my daughter with a total stranger. Then I would feel bad! I'll feed her, put her in the purse, and she will fall sleep. Yes, good. That is how I am going to do it.* A brilliant plan by Luci's mom to be able to get out and have a few drinks and meet some men while at it. She hadn't touched alcohol since that puking incident, but she was craving it so much now. A glass of chardonnay or Shiraz! A fruit martini! *Ummmm, so tasty! Okay, Luci, we are going purse shopping. I love my new doll—oh, not doll! My daughter, Luci! Yes, I love you, my dear daughter, Luci.*

Luci's mama found herself a perfect purse. First she went to a department store and found nothing there. She met a friend in the process, and her friend suggested this shoe boutique in the south part of downtown and gave her the address. Luci's mom pushed Luci's stroller out of the department store and started walking toward the boutique. A beautiful sunny day in paradise! The whole time she was walking, she was thinking of how she was going to sneak Luci into this bar and into that bar. How she was going to react if Luci started crying. She had to find a purse that opened from the top with a zipper. *Oh, my little doll, I will make sure I'll get me a purse that you will be comfortable in. I promise, my little china doll. So fragile*!

Luci was so little, so petite! She wasn't gaining weight from her mom's breastfeeding. Her mom was smoking lots and not eating too much, since she wanted to lose the weight she had gained during pregnancy. So Luci could easily fit inside a large purse even at six months.

Luci's mom found the purse she liked, and at a hidden corner of the store, out of sight, she took Luci out of the stroller and gently put her inside the purse. A bit tight, but she could still move around in it. Great! It worked. She was so excited. *Wow. No one will know. I will make sure she is asleep, and I will just go for an hour or two. Not longer than that*. Luci's mom paid for the purse, looked around the store a little bit more, like all the other women just aimlessly looking at shit they have no interest in or intention of buying. Just killing time!

Guys can never do that shit. The only time you see a guy doing that is when he is with a woman in that store. No other time. Guys, when they are shopping, they are *shopping*. They go shopping with a mission, to buy two, and not three, but two pairs of pants, two to three shirts, maybe a couple pairs of shoes—one sporty and the other dressy—and that's it. Men are done and on their way to do other shit in less than two hours. Women take for-fucking-ever. And they have to go to every store, and honestly there are so many stores catering to women. But the fact remain, with all their bullshit, men still love women, no matter what their sexual preference! Men love women. There are more gay men showing more love to women than straight dudes do. Anyway, that's off the topic. Where were we? Luci's mom.

Home again. Back from the purse shopping that took five hours resulting in purchase of only one purse. Luci seemed to be enjoying herself in her stroller. Looking up at her mom, then at glass doors, colors, big square things and small square things, things dangling! Mommy was saying something to this cute person who kind of looks like Mommy. She looks nice. Mommy looks nice too. Mommy looks really happy. *I am going to smile for Mommy when she looks at me next. Oh, there she goes. I am smiling for Mommy. I love you, Mommy.*

Mommy is taking a shower while Luci is taking a nap. Mommy does not deny anything for her baby. Best of everything! Best crib, best clothes, shoes, hats, gloves, you name it, the best for my baby. *My baby deserves the best. I will find you a daddy. Tonight, when we go to the bar together I will find you the best daddy.*

Sammy is waiting, panting, walking back and forth. Looking at everything like something is hiding somewhere and he has to find it. Everything could have something. Nothing could lead to anything. *Let me look here. Let me look over there. Oh, what is that? Oh, there. I see something there.* Nothing! It was all nothing. Nothing, like his own life! Full of nothing! How did he get here? From many things to nothing! How could he, Sammy, let this happen? *Holy shit! I am nothing.*

Sammy collapses on the sidewalk. No sign of Luci. Where is she? What are these thoughts I am having? It's ridiculous! I have me. I have Sammy. That's everything I need, just me! I don't need anything else! Where is Luci? Oh that extra $10 that I need! Fuck. Where am I gonna get that ten bucks? That bitch, Luci! After all that I have done for her. She won't give me a break on just ten fucking bucks.

Oh, excuse me, sir. Can I please get a quarter please, sir? Please, just a quarter. I need forty quarters to make $10. Okay, let me try again over there.

There are more people passing over there. Sammy frantically talking under his breath and walking fast paces in and around himself! *Oh no, the rain is starting. How am I am going to get the money in this rain? Oh God, please give me a break.*

Just a quarter, please. Please a quarter, please. Oh, thank you, a dollar. Oh, thank you, sir. Thanks. God bless! Wow, a whole dollar. Now I need less than forty quarters. Oh, what is that? Is that a quarter? Looks like a quarter. Let me see.

"Sammy! Sammy! Hey, Sammy! Sammy!" Loud. "Sammy!" Louder.

"Oh hi, Luci. So good to see you, Luci. Oh, Luci."

The rain is coming down in puddles. It's wet and hard and he is getting even more wet! Wetter than wet ever was and is. He runs toward Luci's sound. He really can't see very well, with all the heavy rain blinding him.

He sees her shadow in front of a car. She is in front of this red car. *What is she doing with a car?* Sammy asks himself.

"You have the money, Sammy?" Luci asks.

I am $9 short, Luci. I will beg right here all night to get the money for you, Luci. Please just hook me up, and I won't leave this place until I get your money."

"You are such a fuck, Sammy. You are the biggest fuck I have ever seen. You are shit, Sammy, pure shit. You stay here all night and give me whatever you make, you fuck. Piece of shit! Here, give me what you have." Lucy barks at Sammy while she is grabbing him by his wet shirt collar and looking him right in the eye. He gives her the money and takes the crack and the heroin. He runs toward the alley, where he usually goes to take a hit. *Should I do the heroin first or smoke the crack? Let's smoke the crack and then shoot up, yeah! That's the way to do it!*

Sammy smokes the crack cocaine, a nice-sized rock from Luci, and then after a few minutes shoots the heroin into a spot in his arm. He is running out of spots in his arms and uses his ankle every now and then. Shooting up in the ankle really hurts! Sammy is now really high and slowly going into a deep convulsion of thoughts. Random thoughts just flashing through his mind! *My daughters! God, I haven't seen my daughters for so long. I don't even know what they look like.* More scattered thoughts. *Fuck, this is good shit. Thanks, Luci! I really needed that. Oh, my damn greed. One more hit, one more fuck, one more toke, one more drink, one more this, and one more that. It is always one more.*

"Fuck, I am a greedy bastard," he mumbles to himself and then laughs. The laugh quickly stops, and a flash of a smile crosses his unwashed face and dried lips. He is again thinking about his greed. *Everyone is greedy. I am like everyone else. But I should be able to control it. What the fuck am I talking about? Damn, where is Tony? Oh, my friend Tony. Love you, Tony. Miss you, bud.* He is deep in his thoughts crouched down in an alley under heavy rain. He is feeling cold, but he cannot get up to get out of the rain. He lays beside a Dumpster and covers his face with his jacket. The foul smell of the Dumpster and his body odor annoy him. He always has had a problem with bad smell, and now he is living in it.

"I am better off dead. This is not a life fit for a dog," Sammy mumbles to himself again as he gets up. The rain is getting heavier, and now he is completely soaked from head to toe. His clothes feel very heavy. He looks toward the road and sees a shiny house across the street just like the one he had. There, in front of the house, under the bright light he sees his children standing there watching him. Oh my God, my children have come to visit me. He picks up his steps and runs headfirst toward the light across the street. A delivery truck rams him on his side, his hip snaps on impact, and his frail frame goes flying up in the air. He is so high he has no idea what just happened. His face crashes into the pavement. "Oh my, it's finally gonna be over." Sammy's last words!

Greed! It exists within every human being—everyone, no exceptions. And humans are not or cannot be the only living thing that is greedy. But what the humans have that other greedy living organisms don't have is … *money*. Money! The root of all evil, according to many. It is widely believed that money brings power, and majority of people seek that power! A male lion defending his pride is extremely powerful but has no money. Think about it: one can be powerful but have no money. So money does not necessarily bring power. The male lion defending his pride is more powerful than any millionaire or billionaire. Exchange of money for commodities and services completely changes everything and takes the human greed to a complete different level. We, humans have been taught over and over on mechanisms to want more of that money. Earn more and pay less! That is a definition of a smart person. But have we ever learned to control our greed for wanting more money? Can we control our greed? Is our greed endless, just like the universe we live in? I think *not*! We are capable to control our greed; otherwise, the world as we know it will disappear, all because we would not curb our greed. We need to teach everyone, young and old; hey, let's come up with a lesson on greed control. Let's write books on how to control our greed. We have so many books on how to be greedy and want more — why not books on how to control it? We have every other control. Ground control, crowd control, air traffic control, substance control, and endless other controls. (Hi, reader! If you have more "_____ control," please send them to me.) Let there be textbooks in our schools about greed and how we can control it. It's important for sustaining our future.

Sammy, a man who had everything, died having nothing. Why? Because he wanted more than everything he had. His greed got the best of him and finally took his life. The only perfect things about us humans are our birth and our death. Everything else in between is as imperfect as our lives.

Story 2

Constable Johnson and Fully Loaded

It's time to go to bed. I don't want to sleep, but I *must. I must go to sleep*. There's a busy day ahead tomorrow. Haven't been able to sleep well for a while. I go upstairs and lie in my bed looking up into the ceiling. The white, plain ceiling. How I miss her; and how I don't. The window is open, and I am listening to the sounds of the night under my window. *Sirens*. I hear them coming from afar. It sounds like many sirens, not just one or two but many. The sirens are getting louder and closer. It sounds like they're just around the corner. So loud now. Different sounds of sirens mixing together. Some different from the others, or maybe they were all the same and I heard different! I can't think anymore; the sirens are piercing into my head. The sounds of sirens have taken over my brain. I can't hear or think of anything except the sirens. Insane in the membrane, insane in the brain! I picture them speeding by; the sound does the rest. In a split second the sirens are silenced!

"Driver! Open your door slowly, and put your hands outside the car!" Constable Johnson screams through his speaker mike to the occupants of a blue truck.

Johnson's gun is drawn, and he is using his cruiser's door as a shield in case there is a shooting. His partner is also out of the cruiser, gun pointing at the truck. (Reader, give any gender and name you like to Constable Johnson's partner.)

"I repeat, now open your door and get your hands out of the car … now!"

"*Fuck* you, pig! I am not opening shit, *piggy*! *Fuck you*!" Byron, the driver of the blue truck *croaks* back; the lump in his throat so damn big it cuts off most of his words. It feels like he is choking. He has never been caught before. He has been chased few times but never caught like this with fucking cop cars on each side of him. Fucking guns drawn! Fucking guns, man! Byron feels his gun in his hand. Fuck, it feels so good to just fucking draw this piece and start wailing the motherfuckers. He keeps his gun in a pouch he designed and made which he wears on his big-ass belt.

Byron's a thief; a car thief. He has been stealing cars for the past five years and has never been caught … well, until tonight that is! Byron is known on the streets as FL, which stands for Fully Loaded. Eeff-El. This is how many Persians pronounce the Eiffel Tower: Eeffel. His Persian friends gave him the nickname since he is a tall. Six feet, eight inches and well built. FL has many Persian friends. He enjoys their wisdom, street smarts, sense of style, daring nature, and also, addictively, their women and opium. Yes, he is addicted to the beauty of the Persian women and the serene feeling after smoking opium, Teriyak. Byron is a good-looking guy. Mixed English and Swedish, and a bit of German in him. He is not just a pretty face. He is also a scholar. At the age of twenty-six, he has a law degree, so he is not anybody's fool. But he gets a rush from stealing cars. He looks at it as his expensive and dangerous hobby. They have come close, but he found a way to get away. Like you see in the movies! But FL is for real. He is no movie. Real time, baby! So he went with a street name of FL, but he told everyone it stood for fully loaded. Fully loaded what? Not many people knew or even wanted to know what it stood for. Was he referring to a gun or his cock? *Why does it have to be always either a gun or a cock? Why can't it be the brain or the eyes or a car? Fully loaded! I have seen people fully loaded with their brain power. Smart, fun, and at the same time disciplined individuals! Surround yourself with fully loaded people.*

Constable Johnson has fired his gun only twice outside the firing range. Once he missed and the other time he didn't. He didn't kill the person he hit, but that night in bed he could not get the image of the bloody man on the sidewalk out of his head. It was a gruesome scene. He didn't want to draw his gun anymore. He didn't want to kill. But now, without any hesitation, he opens his holster and draws the gun. The gun feels a bit heavy in his hand! He has this feeling in his gut that he is going to shoot his gun tonight, and he just is not the man to take someone's life. No, not he! A gentle soul but a cop at the same time. Needs to serve and protect but not kill. He has a bad feeling about this one. Now he directs his conversation to the passenger.

"Passenger, be smart and follow my instructions. Open your door, put your hands out, and slowly come out of the truck. We know you are innocent. Don't take a hit for this scumbag buddy of yours." Constable Johnson tries to get through to the passenger.

"Fuck you, pig. We're not listening to you. You are the scumbag, you fucking pig. You want me, pig, then come and get me. I am right here, you fucking scum," replies FL.

"Guys, we can do this the hard way or the easy way. There are more of us here than you guys in the truck, and there are more on their way. Are you hearing the sirens? If you can't, well, I can!" They are coming from every direction. *Holy shit, what is going on?* "We are going to make you come out of that truck, punk! You can bet on that, but how we are going to do it is entirely up to you. Now, what is your decision? Make one right now, and make it the right one and you know damn well which one is the right one." Constable Johnson screams to the occupants of the stolen truck. He figures there are two, maybe three, occupants in the truck. There are six police officers at the scene with their guns drawn. At least four more cars are coming. That's eight more cops in total, not counting the one in the paddy wagon. These guys have no chance of escaping this scene, and if there is any shooting, those guys in the truck are going to be dead. He needs to finish this without any killings. It doesn't look so promising right now.

Johnson is keeping calm, but his patience is running thin. He notices that he is aiming the barrel of the gun right at FL. Right at his head. This kid is too cocky, and he doesn't care. He is not the one wanting to go to jail. *Stay calm. Talk to the passenger.* "One man in the truck is better than two," Johnson says to himself, while his palms get sweaty holding the gun handle ever so tight; his index finger touching the trigger ever so gently. *Fuck, I don't want to shoot this kid. Goddamn it, get the fuck out of the truck.*

FL yells, "Pig! What the fuck? Cat got your tongue? Let me go, pig, and I will forget your face. You have my word. I won't harm you or fuck your wife and children. I will let this one go."

Constable Johnson cannot believe what he is hearing. What is this? A threat? Not really! He is not threatening me. Then, is he forgiving me? Yes, he is forgiving me for stopping him. Fuck this shit. I am going to shoot this son of bitch!

FL made friends wherever he went. His family moved around a lot. From city to city, country to country. He lived in Iran from age ten till nineteen. He got along with the kids at his school, and he was popular with the local kids. The Iranians loved him! He was a handsome young boy and a social butterfly. He also liked girls from an early age, and he flirted with girls his age and some much older. He kissed an eighteen-year-old girl at the back of her family's garden in the suburbs of Tehran when he was also eighteen. He loved every minute of that encounter and remembers it well, like it happened yesterday.

That day FL and his family were invited by this Iranian family to their private garden retreat in the outskirts of Tehran. These gardens were called *bagh*, and this particular bagh had a two bedroom house inside it. This bagh's home had two levels with the bedrooms in the second level. A traditional Iranian architecture with a courtyard in the middle. First floor had the living room, kitchen, dining room and a guest room. A small shallow pool with a fountain in the middle added to the exterior décor of the courtyard. There were all sorts of little fish in that pool. FL loved looking at the fish and trying to figure out what they were thinking and going to do next. He could watch fish for hours without saying a word. He was looking at the fish inside the pool, when he felt someone very close behind him. He turned around, and there she was, standing right behind him, smiling. In broken English she greeted FL, and FL, in broken Farsi, replied *Salaam. Khoobi*? She smiled and started speaking Farsi to FL, and FL continued to speak in Farsi to her in his Canadian accent, which was a bit comical to her. The father of the girl worked with FL's father in a tall building on a very busy street in Tehran. FL used to go and visit his father at his office after school, and they would ride home together. His father had a large office, and he had many people bringing him stuff: tea, fruits, papers, more tea, cookies, more papers. *Oh my favorite fruit Anar – Pomegranate.*

"Oh, you speak good Farsi. Cute accent! Honestly very cute! But can we continue our conversation in English? I like to practice my English with you."

FL told her how he liked looking at the fish and trying to figure out what they were going to do next. She asked him what he thought a fish might be thinking. "I don't know. I don't think fish thinks. Fish just moves on impulse and vibration and not on thought."

"How old are you?" the Persian girl asked with a serious look on her face. FL was tall but had a baby face, and many girls thought he was only fourteen, fifteen at most.

"I am eighteen. In a month I will be nineteen," FL replied coolly, sporting a cheeky smile. "And you, how old are you?" FL asked the most beautiful girl he had ever seen in his life. Just stunning! She was wearing a yellow and red summer dress, hemmed to below her knees, and a very cute hat. It suited her beautiful face. Such a perfect face, with beautiful hazel eyes, a cute tiny nose, and long straight black hair all the way down her back!

"I just turned eighteen," she replied. "Are you having fun here in our bagh?"

"Yes, it is very nice and peaceful here."

"Do you want to see my tree house? I have made a tree house on top of this big tree a few minutes away from the house. It is still in our property, but it's so well hidden no one can find it. Only two people who helped me build it know about it, and they don't dare talk about it with anyone. So what you say? You want to see it?" the Persian girl asked excitedly

FL was at the age now that he was peaking sexually. Looking at nice legs and tits made him feel tingly, which made his penis rise up without any shame. He feels his penis rising upwards while looking at the girl.

"Did I tell you to go up? No! Then why the hell did you do that? Penis replies: I have the mind of my own. Live with it. I will embarrass you now by going up at the most awkward situations and will embarrass you even more when I will not go up however hard you try."

She noticed a bulge in FL's trousers, and she started to giggle which turned into a full blown laugh. He knew why she was laughing, and he felt somewhat embarrassed. He turned around and started rubbing it so it would go down. Lo and behold, rubbing it was not going to make it go down.

"Okay, let's go and see your tree house," FL said all of a sudden, his back to her.

She grabbed his hand and said, "Let's go. This way!"

They left the bagh hand in hand, walking and looking at each other with quick glances. They both knew what was about to happen. Neither of them knew how, but both of them knew it was going to happen. They walked for awhile and then got to the tree line, and she told him the tree house was beyond that. "Come, you will like it." He stood there looking at her, feeling a bit scared. It was getting dark, and the families would be looking for them soon. He had better act right away. He started following her into the trees. They walked a few meters, and she grabbed his hand and put it on her breast. He was shocked with her abrupt action but he was not complaining. He started squeezing her right tit and with his other hand rubbing her long neck. She took off her hat, and her black hair flowed everywhere on his face. He was so much in the moment enjoying himself he didn't even ask about the tree house. (There was no tree house. There never was a tree house.) More squeezing of the tit and playing with her hard nipple! It was time for a kiss. He moved his face toward hers and kissed her on the lips. To his surprise he was pretty good and she as well. It must have been all those movies he watched. They both enjoyed kissing each other, since they were both good at it. After the kiss she giggled and held FL's hand in hers. He felt a bit embarrassed, but all he could do was smile with her and squeeze her hand in his. She stopped smiling and grabbed his face and kissed him on the lips and held him very close. *Wow*, he thought, *she is such a good kisser. Wow! I don't want this moment to stop. Please don't stop.* They kissed for a long time. He was keeping up with her in moving his tongue inside her mouth and squeezing her lips in his. She started rubbing herself more and more on his hard cock. Their breath became heavier and louder. A sudden sound in the bushes!

"What was that?" FL asks.

The sound again!

"Oh, no. It sounds like someone is coming this way."

"Oh, shit. We must run. It could be our parents," FL says to the Persian girl. God, he wanted so much to continue kissing her, but they must run first. They started running away from the sound and then walked a long way back to the house. There was no one at the house. She took FL to her bedroom, and without saying a word, they took their clothes off and had sex. What a beautiful feeling that was for both of them. Each lost their virginity with the other. They gazed at each other and kissed each other for as long as they could. FL left her room and went to the room that he shared with his parents. He lay down on his mattress with the biggest grin. All of a sudden, he smelled her scent on himself. He was just beside himself. Such a beautiful scent! Scent of a woman, intoxicating and addictive! He closed his eyes and went through the whole experience, from the very start when she came into the courtyard and started talking to him. Such a beautiful experience with this lovely girl! *I will never forget this*, FL told himself. Indeed, he never forgot her, but he never again saw her either.

"Driver, stop making threats and come out of the car. Don't make this any more difficult for yourself and us. You are surrounded! You don't want to die! Come out of the car before we force you out," Constable Johnson shouts over his mike. He wants to give this punk another chance. He really doesn't want to kill him. He likes his courage. This kid is too good for himself. Constable Johnson knows very well who he is dealing with here.

Meanwhile, FL has texted one of his buddies who has a very fast, very maneuverable car to come and bust them out. He wants to break free, and he tells the other occupant of the car that this is what he is going to do. "Jap is coming to pick us up. Are you in or out?" FL asks his buddy.

"I am in with you all the way, FL," his buddy replies.

"Okay. Jap is going to be coming down the street right in front of us. He is not too far. He has another guy with him. They are going to come out of the car and start shooting at the cops. As soon as we hear that, we get out of the truck and start shooting at the cops behind us. That fucking pig with the microphone! He is fucking mine to own," FL tells his partner in crime.

Constable Johnson has no idea of the occupants' firepower or if they have any firepower at all. This bullshit episode is dragging on longer and longer and he is not liking it. The streets around this standoff is closed off by other cops, and no one can get in or get out of this hellhole.

"Situation is very tense," Constable Johnson says on his radio.

"Make them come out of that fucking car, Johnson. Should I send someone else to do your job?" the sergeant on duty shouts back into the mike. Johnson can see the sergeant's big-ass mouth coming out of the mike and spitting all over his face. Johnson keeps the mike away from his face. "Fucking asshole," he mumbles under his breath.

"Okay, okay, Sarge. Give me a fucking break. They are surrounded. They cannot go anywhere."

"I don't give a shit where they can go or not go. I want those punks out of that truck and spread-eagle on the pavement with fucking handcuffs on their wrists, you hear me?" Sergeant Asshole screams again.

Fucking asshole! He only knows to scream. No wonder he has been divorced six times, and every time they cleaned him out. Still, the idiot got married. You would think he would get it after the third marriage. But fuck no. Six times.

"Driver, I am losing my patience with you. You're going to come out of the car, or we're going to force you out. I mean *now*!" Johnson shouts with anger.

FL's phone rings and it's Jap on the other end.

"All the roads are closed, FL. We have no way of getting to you. You are surrounded, man. Please save yourself and give yourself up."

Fuck fuck fuck! I am surrounded by these fucking pigs. How the fuck am I going to get out of this one? FL's partner asks him about the phone call. FL doesn't say a word and shuts his phone off. He never shuts the phone off. This time he shuts it off completely.

"What the fuck is going on, FL? Please talk to me, man." His partner's voice is shaken, his tone urgent.

"Get out of the car, my friend. Save yourself. You don't have to do this. Please get the fuck out of the car and give yourself up. They can't pin anything on you. It's going to be all me, and I am thinking of making a run," FL tells his partner while looking him dead in the face.

"I am with you all the way, FL. Don't ask this from me, man," his partner tells FL with a stern face.

"No, don't be stupid. Get out of the car. *Now*!" FL shouts at his partner and forcibly turns him around and opens the passenger door.

"Movement on the passenger side! The passenger door just opened up, and I see the passenger and driver talking without moving a muscle," Johnson calls on the radio. "Passenger, put your hands out where I can see them, and get out of the car slowly," Johnson calls to FL's partner through his PA.

"Go, please go, my friend. Don't ruin your life for me. Please," FL asks his friend and longtime loyal partner. "Go now."

FL's partner is as tall as FL. He puts his hands out and waves them in the air and starts to shift his body very slowly toward the open door, moving forward until his feet touch the pavement.

"Put your hands on top of your head, and slowly go down on your knees, and once down on your knees slowly put your arms in front of you and go down on your stomach and spread your arms and legs. Do you understand me?" Johnson sees there is still hope to end this peacefully.

FL's partner with one quick jerk jumps out of the car and starts shooting his handgun with one hand and his Uzi machine gun with the other, screaming to FL to run. Bullets fly everywhere, and Johnson and his colleagues are crouched behind their metal car doors so they don't get hit with the barrage.

FL comes out of the car running the opposite direction from where his partner was shooting and takes his only weapon, a handgun out and starts shooting over his shoulder while running at full speed. Ta tata tatatatatatatatatatata. Gun fire heard from all sides. Police are not firing back, they are just taking cover. They can't match the firepower of these two guys, specially FL's partner. FL runs to a police car, immediately shoots the cop in the upper leg, gets behind the wheel, and drives away like a maniac. His partner is still shooting, and then *bang bang bang*, he is dropped with three bullets, two to his head and one to his chest. The only fatality of this mad shooting rampage! The person who started it goes down and is the first and the only one down. He is not yet dead and falls face first hitting the pavement hard. The impact crushes his cheek bones and part of his skull. He is barely alive and breathing heavily in short spurts. He sees shadows and shoes moving around him. Voices mumble stuff he cannot understand. *Wow. I don't feel anything.* He closes his eyes, and they never opened again.

FL is driving the cop car, hitting anything and everything in his destructive path. He knows the city very well. He hears sirens and knows very well the cops are on his tail. He has to ditch the cop car and hide somewhere. He drives the cruiser into a park and rams it into a bushy area behind the restrooms. He then jumps out of the car and starts running. He is a fast runner and a good runner as well. He runs every day for few kilometers. One step in front of the other, as fast as he can. He hears a gunshot very close by and immediately feels a sharp pain in his right side. His hand immediately goes there and comes away warm, moist, and sticky. *Fuck, am I bleeding?* Yes, he is bleeding. He was hit by a bullet from a fucking cop. *Who the fuck shot me? Fuckers!* FL doesn't really know where he was shot, but he was shot by a cop who was shooting at his direction and at that moment he had caught FL with one of his bullets.

It's just a flesh wound.

But it isn't. The bullet penetrated his skin was logged inside. He is bleeding from his side, and the blood gushes out of the open wound. He takes off his shirt and presses it on the wound. It's not helping! *Fuuuuuuuuck. I don't need this shit right now.* His legs feel very weak. He is slowing down. *I need to get the fuck out of here.* He could hear dogs barking in distance. The barking is getting closer. *Shit, not the dogs! I can't die here. Not here. This is so shameful for me—no, not just for me, for anyone to die out in this filth. When I die, I want to die at the comfort of my own home, you know what I mean. Not here. I don't deserve this.*

FL's legs cannot take another step. His whole body is shutting down bit by bit. *I am dying. Wow. This is how it feels to die.*

"Son, come here and look at this fish. It is called white fish here in Iran." He can hear his father's voice and see his father's image pointing to the fish. *Where is the fucking fish? I am hallucinating. There are no fish around here. Just me dying!*

He stops moving. His hand grips his injured side, and blood spews everywhere. His shirt is soaked with blood. He can't stop the bleeding, and he sure is trying hard. He can feel the blood leaving his body. Life leaving his body slowly but surely! *I lived a good life. Amazing people I met, and the shit I put myself through. I love my life even if it is leaving me.*

FL falls on the pavement. He does not feel any pain, and this is strange to him. *How come there is no pain? This wound should hurt like a son of a bitch,* but nothing. Absolutely no pain! His father's image comes to him again, talking about goldfish this time.

FL's father loved the goldfish that Iranians kept in the little backyard pools of their homes. So did FL. He basically loved everything his father did. He adored his father.

Most Iranians had this shallow pool in their backyards which was called "Hoz". Most of the pools had a fountain, which they turned on every night in summer to cool the air. These pools were usually full of fish. Different colors of goldfish, big and small! All living and swimming in total harmony, without any conflicts, wars, or destruction. They would bump into one another here and there, but that didn't matter: So what? It's just a bump. Don't take it too fucking seriously, man! The shallow pools were usually made of artistic tiles. The opened fountains would splash water inside the pool and most times when the water shot higher it would splash to the outside of the pool. It was so refreshing and relaxing, the sounds of the water splashing from the fountain hitting different objects.

FL fell into a coma. A long coma, dragging out for just over a month. He doesn't really remember how he ended up where he did, because the last thing he remembers was the fish swimming in the pool and him drifting away with his father's voice calling out his name.

"What's your name?" A voice from nowhere calls on him, and the voice from nowhere startle him. He gets the chills all of a sudden. He feels the goose bumps on his neck and arms. *Am I dead and that's the voice of God asking me my name? Why would God ask me my name? God has such a lovely sexy voice. I always thought God was an old man, not a hot-sounding girl.*

"What the hell is your name?" the sexy voice asks again, but this time with some authority, so he would know who the boss is.

That is no god. Its one pissed-off hot sounding chick, FL thinks to himself. Fuck, who the hell is she?

"They call me FL," he says faintly to the voice. "Who are you and how did I get here?" he asks politely.

At this time FL has opened his eyes but all he sees is black shadows. It's all black around him. He touches his eyes, and there is nothing covering them. He knows and feels that his eyes are open, but he can not see. *Oh no. Oh, fuck no. I can't see. I have lost my sight. What the fuck happened to me, man?*

"My brother brought you here. You were shot. One shot to your body, and you also took a shot to your face. My brother shot you, and then he found you in one of the alleys passed out and bleeding, so he brought you here," the voice says.

"How long have I been here?" FL asks while trying to remember the sequence of events again.

"Over a month. You have been in and out of consciousness for all this time, and I have been nursing you. You were operated on by one of my colleagues to stop the bleeding. Both bullets had exited your body and face." The voice says, still authoritative and straightforward. Not missing a beat and telling it like it is.

"Is your brother the cop?" FL asks, and this time not so politely.

"Yes, my brother is the cop who shot you and then saved you." The voice seems now to come from somewhere else nearby. More hollow than before, as if she is in a tiled place like the kitchen or the bathroom.

"How the fuck did I survive? How did you nurse me? I must have been nearly dead. Why didn't he leave me be? I would have died, yes, but I would have died with my dignity. What am I now?" FL asks, some hurt in his voice.

"A blind, crippled piece of shit who was saved by his shooter and nursed by his shooter's sister."

FL starts laughing, and his laugh grows loud and violent, turning into a cry. A loud and sad cry! Bawling! Tears coming out of the eyes which are blinded, just pouring down his face! He touches his face, and it feels different. *What the hell happened to my face? I will never be able to see what my face looks like now.*

"Was it worth it? Was it worth all this?" the girl asks, and her voice seems to be close as if she is right there. She must be sitting right next to the bed. Next to the bed FL has been lying on for some time now. She smells nice. *Wow, my sense of smell! I could never smell like this before.* FL is taking deep breaths and taking in the many odors that are surrounding him. She smells so divine. It's intoxicating. It's lethal!

FL immediately starts to move his toes and legs. He feels very sore, but he can wiggle his toes and move both his legs up and down, but, man, everything hurts like a ton of bricks has just been dropped on him and, further, each one of the bricks smashed to pieces by a sledge hammer over his body.

"What did you say?" FL asks the voice. What the fuck did she say? What's worth it?

"Was it worth it? All the stealing, car chases, the running around, and now this. Was it worth it?" the girl asks, this time gently.

"I am not sure what it is you are asking me. Are you asking me that if I knew I would one day be blind and crippled by stealing cars, would I have done it? Yes, I would have, because I would have said you are full of shit, that nothing will happen to FL. Nothing! Why are you asking me this, anyway? What's your fucking business? You have me here all tied to this fucking bed, and now you are asking me if it was all worth it? Fuck you, bitch. Fuck you and your fucking brother for shooting me and not letting me die." FL says this at the top of a voice full of hurt.

"You've been through a lot. I will leave you now. I wouldn't try to get up by yourself if I were you. You have not been on your feet for awhile now and are quite weak. If you try to get up, you will fall. You need help at the beginning." The girl calmly ignores his raging words.

"I have made you some food and need to go out to do some shopping. I will be back in an hour." It sounds as if she is gathering things, preparing to leave.

FL doesn't reply. He doesn't want to live like this. This is not a way for any man to live, let alone FL, who is the king of the world. *Fuck this. I am going to find a way to end this bullshit.*

He then remembers his father's words. Only a coward takes his own life in time of despair. *Don't be that coward, FL. You don't want to be that coward, my son.* He can hear his own father's voice talking to him. He answers: *How I wish you were here. I miss you so much, Dad!*

After the students raided the American embassy in Tehran, and there were talks of other western embassies sharing the same fate, FL's father had gathered the family and told them they must leave Iran immediately, that he was arranging for them to board a plane this night heading to Germany and then back home to Canada. He was confident that they would not have any problems but still had to move about in the protection of dark night. Only their shadows could be seen, not themselves.

FL's father was busy packing with FL's mother. FL was in his room gathering his stuff; his father had instructed him to pack as little as possible. He had a collection of Matchbox cars that he loved. It was his pride and joy, as was his stamp collection. Album after album full of original stamps from all over the world. His favorite was the collection of uncancelled original Reza Shah stamps. They were worth lots of money. He was trying to choose which ones to take. He couldn't take them all, and he didn't have the heart to leave some behind and just take a few. How could he choose between such priceless collections? His babies!

He put all the albums in a large school bag and told his parents he would be right back. He suddenly turned back, grabbed a plastic bag, put all his little cars in them, and walked toward the front door of the house.

"Where are you going? It's too dangerous to go out. Don't make me and your mother worry, for God's sake," his father called to him.

"I'm just going across the street to Farhad's home. I am going to give him some of my stuff," FL shouted back as he headed for the large green gate that opened up into the street. He suddenly remembered all the football games he had played with his friends in this yard using the green gate as a goal.

He opened this gate and looked outside; hardly anyone was out. Being inside their homes was safer than being outside. He ran across the street and rang Farhad's doorbell. Farhad really liked FL and was a good friend to him. FL taught him English, and Farhad loved hanging out with him. They went bike riding together, and Farhad would take FL around the neighborhood and introduce him to the other boys and the girls too.

Farhad's mother's inquisitive voice greeted him over the speaker: "Baleh?"

"Hi. This is Farhad's friend from across the street. Can I please see Farhad?" FL spoke politely into the microphone at the doorbell in broken Farsi.

"Baleh, baleh, alaan migam biyad dame dar"—yes, yes, I will tell him to come to the door now—she replied.

FL heard footsteps coming out of the house, the splash-splash sound of Otofuku slippers, which were quite common in Iran back then.

"Come in, my friend," Farhad told FL when he opened the door.

"What are these you have with you?" Farhad asked while trying to look at what was inside those bags.

"Let's go to your room, Farhad. My family and I are leaving Iran tonight. I want you to have these and keep them safe. You never know: I may come back again one day," FL told Farhad.

They went to Farhad's room, and FL opened the big bag and showed Farhad all his stamp albums. Farhad loved FL's stamp collection, and every now and then he would ask FL to show them to him. Each time he would look at them as if it were the first time. He remembered every time seeing something new in some of the stamps. And now he was going to have them? He was speechless.

"Thank you, buddy!" he finally blurted. "You don't have to do this. Why aren't you taking them with you?"

"I can't. I have to take as few things as possible. No time to chit-chat, my friend. I have to go back and help my parents with packing. I am going to miss you, my friend." FL looked down at the Persian carpet he adored. His eyes were full of tears. He loved Iran and the culture and his friends, and now he had to leave them, maybe forever.

Many years later he got the news that Farhad had died in the Iran/Iraq war. He cried for days when he got the news from Farhad's family. He made a makeshift memorial for Farhad in his room, and he would put an original stamp on that memorial every year on Farhad's birthday. He would also talk to Farhad when he needed to talk to someone, and he claimed Farhad always talked back to him.

FL's family boarded the Lufthansa plane at 2:30 a.m. without any problems and arrived safely at Frankfurt, boarding an Air Canada flight that took them back to Canada the same day. The whole time on the plane, FL was thinking about all the good times he'd had in Iran, and he was very sad to be leaving that wonderful life. He knew nothing about his home country of Canada, but his dad assured him he would be okay there.

"Dad, we never went back to Iran after we left, and I have to say I really miss that place. The people, the hustle and bustle, the traffic, and the sounds and smells of Iran." FL is reminiscing about his days in Iran while lying on the bed blind as a bat. He can see the images clearly in his head, but that's all. He now has to learn to see without his eyes, and only with his mind and other senses. There were no sounds in the place he was, and no sounds coming from the outside either. He can only hear and smell the

Under My Window

sight and sounds of Iran in his head. He falls into dreams of his childhood days, playing football with the local boys in his neighborhood in Tehran.

"What has become of my life? I was on top of the world, and now I am bedridden, at the mercy of my shooter and his sister," he tells himself with an uncanny calmness in his voice. "What is going to happen to me?"

FL hears the sound of a door opening and then closing, and footsteps getting closer. It sounds like a man's footsteps, not those of the girl who was talking to him earlier. When she left he could hear the click-click of her high heels on the floor. Who was here now?

"Can you hear me?" the voice calls out to FL.

"Yes, I can hear you. Who are you?"

"My name is Constable Johnson. I am the one who shot you," the reply comes in a calm voice.

FL wants to jump up toward the sound and grab the man and beat the shit out of him, but no muscle in his body is responding, so he just falls out of bed. Constable Johnson moves toward FL and grabs his arm to help him up. FL slaps his hand away with a furious blow, and Johnson drops him back on to the floor.

"I'd rather die on this fucking floor than have you help me. You fucking murderer!" FL shouts at Johnson, his teeth grinding and spit coming out from the corner of his mouth. He has never been this mad in his life, and he wishes now that he is this mad for his blood pressure to go so high that he gets a heart attack and dies.

"My sister prepared you some food. You must be hungry," Johnson says calmly, not acknowledging FL's comments.

"Is there any poison in that food? Because that's the only way I am going to eat that shit!" FL shouts back, still with that ferocious voice.

"I'm going to leave it on the table next to your bed. Sooner or later you have to move those muscles of yours, so I'm not going to help you. I'm going to leave now. My sister will be home soon," Johnson replies calmly.

"Fuck you, pig. Fuck you, your food, and your sister. I will not eat your food or take anything else from you. You should have left me for dead, and you didn't, and now you must fucking pay for your crimes. I am going to make your and your sister's lives a living hell!" FL shouts again toward the voice.

FL hears the footsteps going away from him and then again the sound of the door opening and closing behind Johnson. Again silence! To add to the silence was the killing odor of the food. It smelled so good, and FL was truly hungry. How the hell did they keep me alive? She said I was in and out of coma, so how did they feed him. He touched his arms to see if there are any marks for intravenous. He notices that his sense of touch has been enhanced, like his sense of smell and hearing.

The food smell is getting stronger, and his tummy is now making noise. He wants to eat that food, but that would mean going against his word. He can't go against his word. It will make him look weak.

Fuck being weak. I am hungry, man.

FL starts dragging himself across the floor toward the smell. It is strange that he can actually see the food with his fingers, ears, and nose. He feels, hears, and smells his way around. However, it's very difficult for him to move. His body is twitching and having spasms in different places while he crawls. *Thank God it's not carpeted*, he tells himself. It would be too difficult to pull himself on the carpet. He is close to the smell, but the smell is coming directly from above him now. *How am I going to get up there?* He raises both his hands as far as he can and starts feeling about in the air. His left hand touches something soft, and he continues to feel it. It feels like the sheets on his bed. He is by his bedside. He is not sure how far he has crawled, but it felt like miles. He wonders why he had to crawl so far to get back to his bed when he just fell by his bedside when he tried to move in the first place. FL takes a rest at the base of his bed. Breathing heavily and listening to his hungry stomach growling even harder. Now he is having a headache. He has to get to that food.

Every movement of his body comes with a struggle. His body has not felt this heavy ever. He feels he needs a crane to lift him up and put him on his bed. He grabs hold of the sheets and tries to pull himself up, but no luck. The sheets slide down toward him, since they are not fastened anywhere.

He suddenly feels an arm go under his arm and start pulling him up. FL takes his arm away with a sudden jerk and tells the person to leave him alone. The arm that was going to pull him up felt strong, strong like a man's.

"Is that you, pig? You shot me and now you want to help me up? Get away from me. You wait until I find a way out of here, and I will deal with you."

"Its me. Jap," FL's buddy quietly tells him

"Jap, it's you. Man, am I ever happy to see you. Fuck what am I saying? I can't see you, Jap. I am blind. The fucking cop blinded me."

"I am here to bust you out, FL. Me and the gang knew you were not dead but didn't know where you were being holed up. I followed the cop, and I see him and this girl coming here every day, and the cop usually leaves after a few hours, and the girl stays in. today I see they both are out at the same time, so I thought this was the best time to come and check if you are here, and I'm so happy to see that you are actually here. Let me bust you out, my friend." Jap tries to lift his friend up.

"Jap, I can't fucking move, man. My legs are like jelly, and I can't put any weight on them. How are you going to get me out of here like this?"

"I came alone, FL. I don't think I can carry you all the way down those stairs, man. I'm afraid they may suddenly show up, and we are done," Jap tells FL while lifting FL up to his bed.

"Fuck, Jap, you gotta get me out of here. I want to come after these two fucks."

"I will go and get couple more guys. Don't worry, FL. I know where you are now. Just give me some time. I will be back with more guys, and we gonna bust you out of here."

"Pass me the food, please, Jap. I am really hungry, buddy."

Jap hands FL the bowl of food and tells him it looks really good. FL tells Jap that the smell of the food is killing him, and that he can actually see what is in the food by its smell.

Jap says good-bye and promises to be back when the place is empty again, to get FL. Then he sneaks out as quietly as he came in. FL is happy now that he knows his friends have found him and are going to bust him out of the place. *I hope they don't get caught*, he tells himself as he eats.

"Not bad. This is good food. Maybe I should just stay here," FL tells himself aloud, and for the first time after a long time, he cracks a genuine smile.

"Were you thinking of leaving us?" the girl's voice calls out to him. "Good, I see you're eating your food. I'm glad you like it. There's more if you want." The girl calls to FL now from a distance.

"Fuck you. I'm eating this because I'm hungry. It tastes like cow shit. You are the most fucking horrible cook ever," FL shouts back to her while sticking large spoonfuls of the food in his mouth.

"Who has been here? Somebody has been here," the familiar voice of Constable Johnson now calls from afar.

"Nobody has been here except you and me and him," Johnson's sister replies.

"Don't lie to me, sis. Somebody else has been here. Can't you see the fucking footprints all the way to his bed?"

There were definitely footprints on the hardwood floor that didn't look like high heels or cop shoes. Definitely sneakers!

"Who came to visit you, thief?" Johnson is now on top of FL's bed, screaming into his face.

"Nobody, pig. The only people here are you and your sorry-ass sister," FL replies calmly. "I *wish* I had visitors other than you two fucks."

"We have to move him. His buddies have found him. We can no longer keep him here," Johnson tells his sister.

"Look, pig, if my friends were here, then how come I am still here, hah? They would have taken me out, and you would have come back to an empty bed. Did you think about that, you stupid pig?"

"I have had enough of you calling me pig, you fucking bastard." Johnson comes over to FL again and punches him hard, right smack in the mouth. FL feels a few of his teeth break, and the taste of blood rushes in. FL spits out the broken teeth along with the blood and starts cursing Johnson. Johnson leaves the place and runs down the stairs.

FL curses after Johnson, calling him all sorts of names while spit and blood gush from his mouth.

"You gonna pay for this, you fucking pig. You gonna pay big. You and your sis are dead. Nobody hits FL and gets away with it. Nobody! You hear that, bitch? You still here, right? I am going to bust out of this place and then come after both of you" FL now is screaming in every direction.

"Do you want more food? There is more if you want me to get it for you," FL hears the girl say somewhere from his left.

"How can I eat when your asshole brother busted my mouth? Fuck, he is going to pay for this."

"Suit yourself. If you want any more food, just let me know. I will make some soup; it will be easier for you to eat."

FL throws his plate toward the voice, and the plate hits the floor and shatters. The girl doesn't say anything. FL hears her shoes clicking on the hardwood floor, and doors opening and closing. Suddenly the sound of a vacuum cleaner cleaning up all the broken porcelain. She picks the big pieces and puts them in a garbage bag while vacuuming the rest without a word.

"*Someone* was here. Who was it?" the girl calmly asks.

"I don't know what are you talking about, you silly woman. No one is here except you, me and your lousy, good-for-nothing brother."

"Don't lie to me. I saw someone sneak in here and shortly after sneak out. I saw him. He was an Oriental fellow. I saw him."

"Then why didn't you tell that to your brother, hah? If you saw him, why didn't you tell him?" FL shouts back, this time with anger and hate.

"Because I love you and want you to be free. I want your freedom. Freedom from everyone and everything. Freedom from yourself, me, my brother, and your former life." This time her voice is very close. FL can feel her motions and know exactly where she is standing.

"You love me? What the fuck are you talking about? How can you love me? Your brother is my sworn enemy, and you love me?" FL asks with a cheeky sarcasm.

"All I have in this world is my brother. Our parents were killed in a plane crash some years ago, and my brother and I have become closer since their death. We were not close before that. He always kept his distance from me. He was very protective of me but not supportive. For him it was shameful to agree with me. Our folks' death hit him very hard, and he found himself vulnerable. He started calling me and wanting to see me and be close to me. We would talk for hours when we met. He would tell me stories about you. How you got away time and again. How you outsmarted the cops every time. I would listen to his stories, and by hearing about you I developed a certain attraction toward you. I so much wanted to meet you. I told myself that the chances of one day meeting you were very slim. You are a hard man to catch, and if they caught you, you wouldn't go down without a fight. When he carried you here unconscious, bleeding, and he told me who you were, I knew right there and then that I loved you."

FL is speechless. He doesn't know how to reply to that. What the fuck? There must be something wrong with this girl.

"So you love me and you want me to get away so your freak brother will have something to do with chasing me around again?" FL asks, this time calmly, thinking about his words before blurting them out.

"No! You are twisting my words. I want you to be free. I want you to be free from everything. I want you to get away and go somewhere where he cannot find you. Just get away." There is urgency in her voice.

"And you? What about your love for me? You love me, but you're just going to let me go so easily?" FL asks mockingly.

"You know the saying: if you love someone set them free? Well, that's what I am going to do. If fate has it, you and I will be together again. I just want your freedom. I don't expect you to love me. As far as you know,

I am your enemy. I am the sister of that so-called evil man who has done this to you. How can I expect you to love me back?" She is now sitting on a chair at FL's bedside. She grabs his hand, and he doesn't let go. She rubs her thumb over his hand ever so gently. A woman's touch after such a long time feels so good. She lets go of his hand and gets up from the chair. She wipes FL's mouth and face with a warm, wet towel and cleans his mouth.

"I'll make that soup now." FL hears her leave.

Her hand was so soft, and her smell was ever so lovely. *I bet she is soft all over*, FL thinks. He thinks about her and what she looks like and how good she is in bed. *Why am I bothering with her? She wants me out, and I am going to get out, so why am I wasting my thoughts on her? She reminds me of the Persian girls. So soft, gentle, and caring! At all times wanting to please their men!* He suddenly goes into a dreamland of his past.

After leaving Iran to Canada, FL spent his junior high in a boarding school in Canada and for the change of scenery FL's father sent him to a boarding school in England for his senior years. Senior years of high school were the greatest. He was in a boarding school in the south of England, and after only one year of being there, he was made a prefect. He was surprised by that, because he was a very naughty boy. But he had charisma. Being a prefect meant having power and lots of it too. He would rule over the school now, and girls would be all over him. There were four other prefects, but he was made the Friday and weekend prefect. Friday prefects were legendary and were considered the fun prefects. They were the ones who would go to teachers and ask them to allow fun events on Friday and Saturday nights at school, such as games night and disco. Prefects were selected by the headmaster, schoolteachers, and past prefects. The ones with the most votes got to be prefects. There were always five prefects, and usually one or two of them were girls, since it was a mixed boarding school. The year when FL became prefect, there were no girl prefects, only five guys.

He had the hots for this Persian girl, but she wouldn't give him the time of day. She hung out only with the Persian crew. Even his speaking Farsi did not impress her, until that day he was announced to be a prefect. She liked authority, and none of the Persians made it as prefects, so she now had eyes for him.

"Hey, congratulations on becoming a prefect. All that power now. What are you going to do with all that power?" the Persian girl asks FL.

"I am gonna win your heart, *azizam*." FL, cocky, uses the endearment with a grin.

"I am afraid you may not succeed," the girl replies with putty eyes looking up and down FL.

"I am afraid I already have," he replies, going for her hand.

So soft and ever so gentle her hand is.

"Wake up. Have some food. You have been out for a couple of days. You need your strength." The voice of a woman enters his head. *What? food? What food? Oh, yeah. Back to reality. Have I really been out for two days?*

FL opens his eyes, and immediately notices a difference in his vision. Before that moment it was all black. Nothingness, total darkness! He could only imagine images based on sounds, smells, and touch. But now he sees light and can make out outlines. *What is happening? I better be quite and see what happens. I hope my sight is coming back. It would be so good if I could see again.*

"What's wrong? You seem very agitated. Did you have bad dreams? You were out for a long time and most times you were mumbling. I was getting worried about you." the girl asks.

"No, just feeling more tired. You are right. I need to eat something."

She hands him the soup bowl with a spoon in it. She asks him if he can feed himself or needs her to help him. He tells her to let him be, that he can manage. He can see the outline of the bowl and the tip of the spoon sticking out of it. *Shit, this is so cool. I can see. I better not let them in on it. I am still going to pretend I'm blind.*

FL starts eating the soup while the girl watches him in total silence. She sits there until FL finishes the soup, a very tasty soup of chicken, barley, carrots, and parsley. It actually fills him up, and he starts to feel much better. His cheeks start to warm up, and he feels a surge of good energy going through his body.

"Thank you. That was very delicious. Can I have another bowl, please?" FL asks the girl while holding up the bowl. He feels like Oliver Twist: "Please, sir. I want some more."

The girl is also sharp and grabs the quote from *Oliver Twist*. "FL has asked for more. I am going to give you more soup. Don't worry." She takes the bowl from FL.

FL lifts his head from the pillow and starts to look around the room, moving his head right to left. At right he can make out is an outline of a window and some frames on the wall next to the window. To his left he can't really make out much, since it is mostly open space, with the kitchen and bathrooms out of direct view. He figures he must be in the living room. He lifts his head up more and looks straight ahead. He can see a door frame to his right; the rest is a blank space. The door seemed to be quite far away.

"Anything else I can get you, sir?" she calls FL from the comfort of her kitchen.

"You have any chocolates? I miss the taste of chocolate. Mousse chocolate, if you have any!" FL replies without any hesitation.

"Yes. There is some chocolate in the house. I am not sure if it's Mousse, but it's good chocolate. I will bring it over to you."

Oh, chocolate. How I miss chocolate. FL is a chocolate addict. Fine chocolate, that is! His chocolates come mostly from Switzerland. He fell in love with Swiss chocolate when he was in Iran. His friend Farhad's uncle studied in Switzerland, and he would travel there every year to give or listen to lectures. He would bring Farhad chocolates from there, and Farhad would always share them with FL. The best chocolates ever!

The girl brings three pieces of chocolate to FL in a small bowl. He grabs one from the bowl, and once he puts it in his mouth he knows it is good quality.

"Belgian chocolates! I don't get anything else," she tells FL.

"It's very good. Have you ever had Swiss chocolate? It's as good or even better," FL replies while the chocolate is rolling in his mouth.

"Yes, I have tried Swiss chocolates. They are indeed very good. These are as good but not as pricey."

Wow, when was the last time I had to worry about the price of anything? FL thinks. He always had the best of the best. Best chocolates, champagne, wine, beer, whiskey, cars, whatever. The best always and never a worry about its cost! *I don't even want to think about the day I have to look at prices of things before getting them.*

The girl comes closer to him now, and he turns to face her. She sits down next to him. His eyes are getting better, and now he can see some of her facial features. He can clearly see that she is wearing glasses. *Oh fuck, she is a geek, man. But hey, geeks can be hot too.* She seems to have a nice figure and moves around with grace. The thing FL really likes about this girl is that she wears high-heeled shoes. He can tell by the clicking sounds they make when she walks around the apartment. Flat, boring shoes don't make any sounds.

"I am going out for a couple of hours. If I come back and you are not here, I understand. I wish you all the best," she tells FL while walking toward the front door.

"Don't worry. I will still be here when you come back," FL replies. His voice is calm for a change.

"Why? Don't you want to get out of here? Don't you want to be free?" She is clearly surprised.

"I am not ready to leave yet. Go and do your thing. I will leave when I am ready."

FL feels a certain attraction toward this girl now that he knows she is in love with him. He hasn't felt like this since the love of his life died of cancer a few years back. Her death was devastating. He proposed to her while standing on a rock off the coastline at the park. FL remembers that day very well, the day he proposed to his love. They were walking in their favorite park next to the Pacific Ocean. They were talking about their future together. He, all of a sudden, hopped lightly over the seawall and ran toward this big rock sticking out of the water. He quickly climbed the rock and shouted over to her, "My love, would you marry me?" He remembers the shocked look on her face when he popped the question. He didn't get an answer right away, since the poor girl was in total shock. He repeated the question thinking she probably did not hear him, this time much louder. By this time people had stopped and gathered around FL's love, waiting to hear what her answer was. "*Yes!*" she shouted loudly, so loudly the word *yes* echoed throughout the park. "Yes! I would love to marry you," she shouted back at FL, this time even louder. The gathered crowd gave out a big cheer and congratulated the bride-to-be. FL ran back to her and embraced her, lifting her off her feet and twirling her in big circles. The crowd was clapping and cheering and patting FL on the back. FL noticed one of the guys in the crowd was John Travolta, on roller blades. FL went over to him and introduced himself and shook John's hand and thanked him for his well wishes and then did one of the signature dance moves from *Saturday Night Fever*. John smiled and moved on while waving good-bye.

FL's fiancée was later diagnosed with an inoperable brain tumor, and six months later she died peacefully in her hospital bed. FL's life was turned upside down. The loss was unbearable, and for the longest time he left his apartment only to get groceries. He locked himself in, away from everyone. FL, the man of steel, was finally broken. He would cry for hours while looking at her picture. From then on, he decided to close his heart to love.

He could not let himself go through that pain ever again. He never fell for another woman after the death of the only woman he had ever loved. Not until now. *I must kill this feeling inside me. I don't want to be in love with her or anyone. Love hurts!* But then he remembers this line from an older African American man, who said, "Where there is love, there is hurt. Accept it." Being in love is such a great feeling. Love empowers you and when in love anything and everything is possible. When in love there are no obstacles. Sky is the limit when you are in love. But love also hurts. When the love of your life leaves you, there is no hurt worse than that. You would rather be hurting from broken legs and arms than a love lost.

"I am back. Did you miss me?" the girl calls.

"As a matter of fact, yes, I did. You are the only person I can talk to. Someone who talks with me without any prejudice. I like that."

"You know I like talking to you. You know that because you know I love you.

Have you ever been in love, FL?" she asks.

"Yes, I have. As a matter of fact, I was remembering her while you were gone. I was remembering the day I proposed to her."

"Did you marry her?"

"No. didn't get that far. She died six months after she said yes. To this day I still miss her."

"I am so sorry for your loss. It must have been really hard on you. I cannot imagine the pain you must have gone through." Her voice sounds heavy with emotion, and FL picks up on that right away.

"Are you crying? Don't cry. She is in a better place. That's what I think anyways," FL says consolingly.

"Do you really believe she is in a better place? Do you believe in heaven and hell?" the girl asks while trying to sound normal and at the same time wiping tears from her eyes.

"I only believe in heaven, and not hell. I believe if there is such a thing as heaven when we die, then it must have different levels. If you have been good and have done good in your present life, you go to a higher level in heaven; and if not, you go to a lower level. I don't believe in fear. Hell is all about fear. That's the only function of hell."

"So, are you saying even the worst of the worst goes to heaven? Then you say there is no punishment in the afterlife for your crimes in this life? That's very convenient."

"That's not what I said. I said there are levels in heaven, and if you are no good, you start at the bottom. Let us say someone committed the most hideous crime, like rape or the gruesome murder of children. Once this person dies, he goes to the bottom, the bottom level in heaven. There he is punished for his crimes, but not with fire, snakes, and scorpions. No. Instead, he is punished by reliving his crime. By seeing how his crime destroyed the lives of people affected by what he has done. He will share their pain and suffering. He will share their hurt every day, over and over again. Once he has endured as much pain and suffering as his victim and his victim loved ones, then and only then he can move up a level," FL explains

"So don't you think that's a very just punishment compared to burning in hell for an eternity?" FL asks, since the girl is completely silent.

"I am thinking about what you said, and somehow it makes sense. I only believe in chi, and I believe when we die, our souls become part of overall energy in the universe, and that's how new life is created, through spiritual energy."

"That's a valid theory also. I like it. I just don't believe in the mumbo jumbo religions trying to feed us bullshit regarding heaven and hell, how these religions create fear in us about suffering for eternity in hell." FL looks straight at her. He can see better now and can make out more of her facial features. She is not the prettiest girl he has ever seen, and he has seen and been with many, but there is something about this girl that is quite attractive and different from other girls. What it is, he cannot yet make out.

"What are you looking at?" the girl asks, jumping from her seat.

"Nothing. I am just looking toward your voice. Is that okay?" FL quickly replies.

"I don't know. It seemed you were looking at me in a way that you could see me."

"No, I cannot see you. Remember? I am blind. Your good brother did this to me." FL replies, again very calmly. He doesn't want the girl to know he can see now. He is not sure how she is going to react, so it is better to keep a lid on it for the time being. He changes the subject.

"I'm hungry. Can I please have some food?"

"What do you want to eat? I have soup and soft chicken pot pie, both homemade." She gets off her chair and walks toward the kitchen. She has a great figure. Long legs and a beautiful straight back! Her hair is long and shiny, and to top it all off, she always smells nice. *This girl really takes care of herself,* he thinks. *I like that in a girl.*

"Can I have soup and pot pie together? I am very hungry."

"Sure. Give me few minutes to warm them up for you. Do you need help feeding yourself?"

"Yes, please. I need your help for sure." He rests his head on the pillow.

FL closes his eyes and goes into his dreamland again. His dreamland was and is and will always be his comfort zone, where no one can enter and harm him. His dream land is his memories, some good and some bad. This time he is remembering the time he had just returned to Canada and was attending junior high in this trendy public school. At that time there were just a handful of Iranian students at the school. He befriended a couple of them, but the rest were reluctant to be friends with him. The ones who didn't befriend him had major trust issues. It was funny; the feeling was mutual: FL felt the same toward them. The two guys became his best friends in junior high before he took off to England for his senior years. They remain good friends. He loves those guys. They are solid and very loyal. He loves this about Persians. When they are good, they are really good. He remembers stealing his first car with them and going for a joyride to Whonnock Lake out in the suburbs. It was an older-model Mercedes, and it was in great shape. The car belonged to one of the Persian boys' neighbors. It was locked in the man's garage, and he would use it only once in a while, and only on nice sunny days. He never, ever took it to work. That day it was nice and sunny, and the boys had just started their summer holidays. In the coming fall, FL would be going to England and this was their last summer to really live it up before separating for a while and getting ready for college and the beginning of a new chapter in their lives. They stole the car and took it to the lake and returned it before the man came back home from work. He had his own shop, so he would be at work from dawn to dusk, and dusk at that time of year is well into the late evening. They picked the lock on the garage door. FL knew how to start a car without a key. It was so much easier on older cars. They took the car out of the garage and closed the garage door and sped toward the lake. None of them had a driver's license, and they didn't care if they get caught. They felt rebellious. They knew if they got caught, they would get away with a slap on the wrist, with some embarrassment for their parents. Boys will be boys, so why not? They were careful driving on major routes, so as not to cause any suspicions. Once they finished their business at the lake, they cleaned the interior and exterior of the car before bringing it back and parking it in the garage exactly the same way it was parked when they stole it. It was such a rush driving that distance back and forth with a stolen car and no driver's license. You have to have some serious balls to pull something like that. Exciting! FL was so excited from the events of the day that he hardly slept that night. He wanted to do it again tomorrow: boldly steal a car in daylight and go for a joyride. That day at the lake, they met some girls and promised them they would be back again the following day. They were fun girls. Suburban girls are always more fun than the city girls. If they like you, they get it on.

The following day he didn't hear from his Persian friends and got a bit worried. He talked to them pretty much every day, but that day nothing. He called both of them, but no one answered at their place. What the hell had happened? He didn't hear from the boys till dark. They were fine and purposely hadn't answered their phones. They were monitoring the neighbor to see if he was alarmed in any way regarding his car. That day, the neighbor drove off with the Mercedes instead. The neighbor returned an hour later and switched cars. He took off to work in his minivan and returned home as usual at 11 p.m. The boys told FL all this and asked him if he wanted to take the car again tomorrow to go back to the lake. FL answered, "Hell, yeah."

The following day they broke into the garage again, stole the car, and headed to the lake. They passed few police cars on the way, and thankfully they didn't hit any snags. The girls were at the lake but were pissed off the boys stood them up the day before. The boys made up all sorts of funny excuses: my dog ate my car keys, I had the runs all day and couldn't get out of the house, my mother tied my leg to my bed so I didn't go out that day, and so on. The girls were laughing hard at all these ridiculous, outrageous excuses. The boys parked their butts right next to them and held the girls in their arms. Before long the boys and the girls were embracing and kissing. FL, lying on his bed, was making kissing faces.

"Who are you kissing?" The girl breaks into his daydream, and she is laughing now. "Your kissing face is really funny. Sorry, I can't help it. It's so damn funny." She is laughing and talking at the same time.

"I was pretending that I was kissing you," FL replies without hesitation. *What the fuck did you just say, you stupid idiot?*

The girl comes over and gives him a nice kiss on his lips. He kisses her back passionately, and immediately they embrace hard. Instantly, they are all-out kissing. Her tongue feels cool and moist, and, man, she knows how to roll it inside his mouth. She is a great kisser.

"You are a good kisser, even with missing teeth" she tells FL, kissing his face.

"You too! Kiss me again." FL brings his lips to hers one more time. They lose track of time kissing. When they hear keys turning the front door lock, they part very quickly. The girl gets up and walks toward the kitchen. The door opens and Johnson walks in. He immediately directs his eyes at FL, who is covered with lipstick marks on his lips, cheeks, and forehead. Pink lipstick! Johnson's sister's favorite.

"What's going on here? How come you got pink lipstick all over your face?" Johnson asks FL.

"Your sister kissed me. I asked your sister to kiss me, and she did. Actually, I didn't just ask her; I begged her to kiss me. I miss my girlfriend's kisses. I miss a woman's kiss, and she did this favor for me and kissed me. I am very grateful to her for doing that," FL replies.

"Did you really kiss this criminal? Did you enjoy kissing this man, sis?" Johnson asks his sister.

"Yes, I did kiss him. No, I didn't enjoy kissing him. As he said, he begged me for it. I really felt sorry for him, so I gave him a few kisses. I feel gross for doing that, but, as I said, I felt sorry for him," the girl replies very calmly.

Johnson buys into the story, since the look on his sister's face is one of disgust and not pleasure. He tells his sister to not feel sorry for this criminal and not to do any more favors for him. He also tells FL to stop manipulating his sister and stop asking her for such stupid favors. "Don't put my sister on the spot, you asshole. She is trembling right now, and that's your entire fault," Johnson shouts at FL. FL recognizes how smoothly the girl covered for both of them and played along. At that precise moment, he realizes how true this girl's love for him is. She did well.

"Has he eaten anything today?" Johnson asks his sister.

"I'm warming up some food for him right now. It should be ready in few minutes."

"Okay. I want him to eat well in the next few days. Get him out of bed and walk him around to strengthen his legs and body. I'm going to move him to a friend's farm in the interior and let him be there for a while. I'm not sure what I really can do with him right now, and I just can't leave him here for much longer. I think I'm being followed, and I'm not sure by whom—his people or my people. I can't turn him in, since I pronounced him dead. What do I even say even if I do turn him in or someone finds him alive here in my sister's apartment? That I have kept him all this time in my custody? By law, that is considered kidnapping. I don't know what to do, sis," Johnson whispers to his sister, looking much stressed. His eyes are bloodshot, and he has grown a rough beard. He never grew a beard. He was always clean shaven. What a mess he has gotten himself into. A big one, that's for bloody sure.

"Why don't you just let him go, my dear brother? Set him free."

"What you mean, sis? Let this criminal walk free after all these years of hardship running after him? Let him go after all he has done and the lives he has endangered with his actions? I have him in my custody after all these years, and now I let him go?" He looks at his sister with an expression that says, *Are you fucking kidding me?*

"Yes, let him go—just like that. You have done what you set out to do. You caught him. You caught him in action, and you also shot him. You could have let him die, and that would have been the end of it. But you didn't. You let him live. You gave him a second chance in life. Why did you do that, my good brother? Have you asked yourself that question? Why did you let him live?" She says that to Johnson while holding his hand and gently caressing it, providing him some comfort.

"Let him go, please. Let him live again. Give him a second chance so he can choose a different lifestyle. He is blind now, and I doubt he would go back to stealing cars and racing them around town in his present condition. You have to let go, my dear brother. I know it's going to be hard, knowing he is out there, but you have no choice. Looking at the situation, you have run out of options." She tells her brother this quietly, so FL can't hear any of the conversation.

"I wish it was that easy, my dear. But you are right! I have run out of options. I can't keep him like this here much longer without someone finding out sooner or later. I also can't report that he is alive and in my custody, because it's against the law, and I could ruin my life with it. How ironic it is that the man I have been chasing all these years is lying a few feet away from me and I have no choice but to let him go free. Wow. This would make a great story one day. Maybe when I retire I will write about this and use fictional characters so no one would know," Constable Johnson tells his sister, and on that note he gives her a hug. He tells her not to mention anything to FL about their conversation just now. He is not sure how FL will react if he finds out he is going to be free. He may get violent and turn on them and hurt her, since he doesn't have anything to lose.

"Don't worry, my dear brother. I'm not going to say a word to him. I have to get his meal ready now." She lies, knowing she is going to tell FL everything, and if he does turn on her, then this is a chance she is going to take. But she is not going to do it just yet. She is going to strengthen him up before she lets him know of her brother's decision.

Meanwhile, FL is trying very hard to eavesdrop on the conversation. He can make out only some words, and whatever he can does not make sense. *Trouble, what to do, live again, second chance, racing them ...* what does all this mean?

"Good-bye, criminal. I'll be back soon. My sister is going to beef you up. You got to move around and get your legs and body back into shape. You're going to need it," Johnson shouts at FL from the front door.

"Why, pig? Why do you want me to get my strength back? So you can chase me again and shoot me down like the coward that you are? Or you want me to get my strength back so I can shit-kick you for what you have done to me?" FL shouts back with equal intensity.

Johnson leaves without a reply. "If I can only get the chance to fight you, FL, I will be the one who will be doing the shit-kicking. I welcome that opportunity any day my man. Any day, any place." Johnson mumbles these words while he goes down the stairs toward the main exit. Once he leaves the building, he notices a couple of people are peering around the corner at him. One is Oriental-looking, and the other one looks Italian. They must be FL's posse. They sure don't look like cops!

"So, what were you guys talking about back there?" FL asks the girl as soon as Johnson is out the door.

"Just brother/sister stuff. Doesn't concern you!" She changes the subject. "Do you have any brothers or sisters?"

"No, I'm the only kid. Seriously, what were you guys talking about? I heard some of it, and I just can't help wondering whether the entire conversation was about me. Hey, no secrets, okay?" When he first woke up from his coma, his very first conversations with the girl were loud, rude, and intense. But now he is calm and very lovey-dovey.

"Why do you think everything is about you? As I said, it was a brother-to-sister conversation and did not concern you. Now your food is ready, and I'm going to bring it over and help you eat it. Please, no more nonsense talks, okay?"

"Don't get upset. Okay, sorry. Are you going to eat with me?" FL knows the conversation was about him, but he is not going to push her anymore. If this is a good thing, he doesn't want to mess it up.

"Yes, I'm going to eat with you. I hope you like the soup. It's the first time I've made squash soup. I got the recipe from a good friend."

"I love every kind of soup. My favorite soups are French Onion, tomato and mushroom. I also like this soup called aash, which is from Iran. It's really good," FL replies.

"Aash? What's in it?"

"All sorts of legumes, such as chick peas, fava beans, and common pea, with vermicelli noodles. It is so tasty. They also add dried parsley. Yum. God, I want aash right now!" FL cries.

"I have some Iranian friends. I will ask them how to make aash, and I will make it for you."

"My dear, it will take years to master the making of aash. It is not an easy thing to make and needs a lot of attention. I have seen it being made, and if you decide you want to make some, I will help you out."

"Okay, let's eat. I'm hungry now."

"Can I get a kiss first?"

"Didn't you hear what my brother said? *Do not manipulate my sister, convict*!" She says it mimicking her brother's authoritative voice and laughs.

She comes over to FL and gives him a long, passionate kiss. Then she brings their food to the table next to his bed. FL carefully sits up and searches the table with his left hand for the bowl of soup.

"Be careful. It's hot. Let it cool down a bit," she tells him quickly.

"Tell me a story while I'm waiting for my food to cool down. Tell me how I looked when he first brought me here."

"Why should I tell you a story that is going to make you sad? I will tell you one day how you looked when you got here, but not today. Let me tell you a story about me growing up with my brother. When we were kids, we played with the neighborhood kids, and the most common games were cowboys and Indians or bank robbers and cops. My brother would always be either the cowboy or the cop, I would always play the hostage either taken by Indians or bank robbers for him to rescue and be a hero."

FL reaches again for his soup, and the girl helps him by bringing the soup bowl closer to his hands. He grabs it and brings a spoonful of soup to his mouth. It's still a bit hot, but that's how he likes his soup: *hot*. He takes the first mouthful, and, man, is it ever tasty soup. It is tomato soup, and he hasn't had a tasty one like this for a long time.

"This is delicious. Did you make this yourself?"

"Yes, from scratch. Just for you, my love!"

FL is enjoying the soup and wondering what the future with this girl has in store for him. He cannot find anything wrong with her. She is loving, caring, and good-looking, has great legs, and most amazing she loves him. *What else do I want from a woman?* he asks himself.

"What are you thinking?" she asks him after watching him sip the soup in absolute silence.

"I am thinking about life with you." He reaches out and finds her hand, presses the back of her hand to his lips, and kisses it.

"I think life will be very good with you. It will be different from a life I knew, but I am sure I can easily adapt to a wholesome, trouble-free life with you."

"Who said anything about trouble free?" she smirks. "I like trouble, and your middle name is trouble."

"What do you mean by that? I'm not sure I understand your point. Are you joking?" FL asks.

"Yes, I am totally joking, my love. I would love a quiet life with you, just you and me and the world."

"Okay, good. I thought maybe you wanted me to go back to my old ways."

"I can't and don't want to stop you from doing anything you want to do. If that's the life you choose once you are out of here, I accept it, because I love you for you and not for what you do." She leans over and kisses him on the cheek. FL grabs the girl and kisses her hard on her lips. They kiss passionately for a long time. She takes off her top and lets him touch her bare breasts. Her breasts are firm and fit perfectly in his hands. Her nipples are hard and feel amazing between his thumbs and index fingers. He keeps rubbing the breasts while kissing every inch of her neck. He is very aroused now and really wants to have sex with this girl, but something tells him to stop.

"Not here, not now. I want it to be special with you. Please, not here," FL tells the girl and pulls away.

She immediately puts her top back on and takes the dishes back into the kitchen. He lays his head back onto his pillow and closes his eyes. In his mind he is replaying what just happened. He really wants this girl in every way, and he hopes he does not disappoint her and himself at the same time by going back to his old ways. She said she will accept him even if he does, but he doesn't want to anymore. He doesn't want to have to run again and maybe one day be arrested and not see her for a long time, not be able to touch her. He is very much in love with this girl.

FL and the girl carry on with their daily routine of getting out of bed and walking around the apartment for few weeks. They share more intimate stories about one another and fall in love even more with each other.

After few weeks Constable Johnson shows up again, and this time he is not as hostile as the other times. He takes his sister to her bedroom and closes the door.

"I've found a way to jail this convict and not get into trouble. I think it will work," Johnson tells her.

"How are you going to do that, my good brother? As soon as you take him anywhere, he's going to tell them that you have kept him hidden for this long, at my place. Tell me brother, what will happen to us once he talks?"

"I'll have his sentence reduced by five years if he doesn't talk. A couple of years in jail, and he will be out. I am going to tell them that he is not the main guy and is one of his assistants. He will go to jail for a short time, and I will have my satisfaction that he served at least two years in jail. He has to pay for his crimes, my dear sister. I just can't let myself set him free. I just can't."

"So are you going to tell him this? What do you think his reaction going to be?"

"Yes, I have to tell him, because I'm going to need his cooperation on this. I'm going to tell him that the maximum he is going to be locked up for is two years, and then he is a free man. No questions asked. The DA is in agreement with this. The DA is my good friend, and he knows the situation. He's willing to cover up for me. He owes me a couple of favors. He is the only one, besides you, who knows of his true identity."

Without waiting for a reply, Johnson opens the door and walks toward the bed where FL is lying.

"Hey. How are you doing today?" Johnson asks FL.

"How come you are so interested in how I am doing, pig?" FL replies tensely.

"Listen, I'll come right to the point. I'm going to take you out of here. I'm taking you to jail. You're going to serve at maximum of couple of years in jail, and then you're a free man. I've made a deal with the DA. I'll make up false identity for you, as one of FL's associates. FL is dead, okay? You as FL are dead. You are a new person now, and in order for that to happen, I must arrest you and put you in jail." Johnson blurts this out very quickly and moves away from the bed.

FL is surprisingly quiet, and he does not say a word for a while.

"I have to think about this, constable," FL finally replies to Johnson.

Johnson, taken aback, is thinking to himself that this went better than he had expected.

"Okay, how long do you need to think this over?" Johnson asks.

"Give me till tomorrow. So you're saying I will only be in jail for a couple of years at the most, no fines, no nothing after that? Nobody is coming after me for any money and bullshit after I am out?" FL asks.

"You will be out with a brand-new identity, and no one will come after you. Guaranteed!" Johnson replies.

"Okay, I will give you an answer tomorrow."

Johnson leaves without saying another word. He is so proud of himself and FL at the same time. FL has definitely changed his tune. He didn't argue, fight, curse—none of that nonsense. He wants to think about it. *I like this new attitude*, Johnson thinks. He leaves the apartment building after looking each way carefully, making sure no one is peering around any corner. As soon as he leaves, Jap and another fellow follow Johnson very quietly and discreetly to where he has parked his ghost cruiser. Johnson is opening its door when he suddenly feels the sharp tip of a knife poking him from each side. Two knives poking him hard!

"Don't turn around. Listen to me, cop," the voice says. "If you love yourself and that girl in the apartment, you gonna listen to what I have to say. You are going to let our friend go free. We know he is in there, and we are watching you at all times. We will fucking kill you if you don't set him free." The voice adds, "We're going to leave now. You count very slowly to twenty, and then turn around. If you turn around right away, we each have a container of acid in our hands and will splash you with it. Here is a bit of demonstration, so you know we are not kidding, cop." The voice instructing Johnson is stern and has a touch of an accent.

They turn his right palm and put a couple drops of acid on his right hand. It starts burning right away, and the pain is unbearable. The pain is suffocating him. The guys withdraw their knives and turn around and start running. Johnson collapses by his cruiser's door, holding his right hand and screaming in pain. A kind of pain he has never experienced before. It feels like a concentrated flame slowly burning the same spot over and over again, going deep into the flesh.

Passersby hear his screams and come over to see what is going on. His palm where the acid was dropped is scabbing. Skin has lifted and flesh is showing. One of the passersby calls an ambulance and stays with Johnson. More of Johnson's colleagues show up and start firing questions:

"Who did this to you? Do you know them? Were you targeted? Did you see their faces? How is the hand?"

"I don't know who they were. I don't know. My hand hurts. Please, I need help here." Johnson is still screaming while trying to reply to his colleagues' questions.

"Anyone called an ambulance yet?" one cop shouts out, and he hears many yeses from different directions.

FL and the girl hear all the commotion happening a block or two away, and then the ambulance siren getting closer and closer and louder and louder. And then it stops.

"I wonder what went down," he says.

"I don't know. I'm going to go down there and see what happened. I have a bad feeling, FL."

"What do you mean? Your brother? You think something happened to your brother?" FL asks.

"I don't know. He just told me about these people who are following him around and are hanging around the neighborhood. He didn't know if they were your guys or his. I wonder if something happened to him. I'm going down to make sure." She opens the door and runs out of the apartment. She sees the ambulance and runs toward it, where many people are gathered and giving instructions. What is going on? She gets closer, and then a male officer asks her where she is going.

"Anyone hurt, officer? My brother just left my place and is not answering his phone. I just have a bad feeling in my gut."

"Who is your brother?"

"Constable Johnson. He just left my apartment, like five minutes ago."

"Oh, lady! It's your brother who is hurt. Someone dropped some acid on his hand. He is going to be okay, but he is in lots of pain." The cop then moves away toward another pedestrian wandering around the scene.

The girl breaks down in tears. Cops would not hurt him with acid. It had to be FL's men. *Oh, my God. I don't know what to do anymore. Please help me.* She cries out and covers her face with both hands, sobbing nonstop. She runs back to the apartment. She doesn't want to see her brother in agony. He is in good hands now, and they are going to take him to the hospital.

She walks into the apartment, throws her jacket on the couch, comes over to FL's bed, slaps him hard across the face, and starts crying. She collapses on top of FL and lets out a loud cry. Then she pushes her face into the bed covers, right by FL's legs.

"They, whoever they are, hit my brother with acid." She sobs and talks at the same time. "I don't know the details. I only know they splashed his hand with acid. He is being treated by the medics, and they are going to take him to the hospital."

FL knows immediately when he hears the word *acid* that it was the work of Jap and the crew. Acid works very well and is not messy. A drop here and there, and the victim is in too much pain to retaliate.

"Do you know if your guys had anything to do with this? Did you order this, FL? Tell me the truth, damn it, did you?" She screams at FL for the first time ever. He has not seen this side of her, and he knows then and there that this girl will kill for her honor and family.

"It was my guys, but I had no idea about this. I didn't order anything. I have no way of contacting any of these people, so how could I have ordered it?" He speaks calmly in order to calm her down.

"I believe you. I'm sorry for hitting you. I was so frustrated, and you are the only one here. You're the only one I could hit, knowing well you are not going to hit back."

"It's okay, my love. It's okay." FL grabs the girl's hand and rubs it gently. "He will be okay. Don't worry about him. His hand will recover," he adds to comfort her.

The girl rises all of a sudden and runs to her bedroom and closes the door. FL can hear different sounds coming out of the bedroom. Closet doors opening and closing, zippers opening and closing, clothes hanger and bathroom sounds. The sounds indicate the girl is packing something. *Is she going away now? Is she going to leave me here by myself?*

"What are you doing, girl?" FL shouts out toward the door.

He gets no reply, and after a few minutes he repeats the question. Again, there is no answer from the girl. Her bedroom door opens, and she comes out with a couple of suitcases and a smaller bag.

"We are leaving, FL. You and I are going to leave this place and never coming back," she shouts out at him boldly and drops the bags and runs toward FL's bed.

"Don't act so hastily, dear. Just calm down! We can't be leaving right now. Your brother is in a jam and needs our help. I don't think we are going to be helping him by leaving. He is not going to like it if I take his sister away without saying good-bye. He would then think I kidnapped you, and things might get worse. I'm seriously thinking about your brother's offer. If I take it, I don't have to run anymore, but if I don't, I have to be on a run for the rest of my life. I don't want that. I want to have a stable life with you and start a family. I don't want to look over my shoulder every time I leave my house."

"I am not going to let you go to jail, FL. We will get out of here and leave the country. Go somewhere that they can't find us. Somewhere in South America. I have money. Lots of money! My parents left us a hefty sum of money when they passed. I haven't used that money for anything. We can take it and leave and start our lives together. Please listen to me. God knows what is going to happen to you in jail. Two years is a long time, my dear. I will not be able to live alone without you for two years!"

"Money is not an issue. I have money, and lots of it, too. I promised your brother to give him an answer by tomorrow, and until now I was going to have him arrest me and I would serve the time. I have done bad things, my love. This is my chance to make good with the world of karma. I need this punishment. I need to make things right again, and if I run, I'm not going to make anything right. I love you and want to make a fresh new life with you. This is why I have to do this."

"Two years? You are going to be away for two years. Is this fair to me now? What happens to me if you decide differently when you are out of jail? What happens to me if you don't love me any more when you are out? What happens to me if they kill the feeling of love in you inside prison? I will die. That's what will happen to me. Do you want my blood on your hands?" She is sobbing hard now and standing her ground. She is not budging an inch.

"I'm sure your brother is not going to be around here tomorrow. Can you please give me till tomorrow to think about this?" FL asks.

"Tomorrow is too late, FL. I know my brother. Before you know it, this place will be crawling with cops. He's going to tell them everything. I know him. He's not going to care if he is going to be in hot water for keeping you here. You will go to jail, and for a long time, FL, not just for two years. After what happened to him he is going to make you pay." The girl tells this fib in order to scare FL, so he will change his mind.

"Really? He will do that. Shit. You know your brother. If he does that, we're all in trouble. Let's get the hell out of here then. Please help me get changed." To the girl's relief, FL hurriedly gets out of bed.

Johnson, in the ambulance, is suffering from the worst pain he has ever experienced. Paramedics are attending to him patiently, pumping him with morphine and bandaging his hand. A friend and colleague is in the ambulance with him.

"What happened there? You can tell me, buddy. Your secret is safe with me." He tells Johnson.

"Bunch of fucking kids who don't like cops, I guess. They ambushed me from the back with knives and told me I'm a disgusting pig and I work for a pigsty and that I should quit and get a real job and then they drop some acid on my hand and run away."

"Kids, huh. Kids have a beef with us? Why you, though? Out of all the cops in this town, why did they have to target you?"

"I don't know, buddy. I guess they saw my ghost car parked in the alley and they thought of me as good bait. They probably said to themselves, *Look, a copper we can fuck with*," Johnson replies.

He wonders how he is going to show up tomorrow to hear what FL has to say about his offer. Will he even be there?

With the help of the girl, FL is out of his bed and in the girl's bedroom, trying on some clothes that belong to Johnson. The girl finds him a shirt and a pair of pants that fit him well and after trying out the clothes he asks the girl to put a couple more pants and shirts into her bag. FL has had neither a haircut nor a shave. He looks like his all-time hero John Lennon when he was in bed with his wife Yoko protesting for peace.

"I look like John Lennon now. I love it," FL tells the girl.

"Excuse me, but how do you know what you look like?" the girl asks FL.

FL is caught. He can't deny that he can see clearly now. His vision is completely back, and he longer wants to play the blind guy.

He turns from the mirror and looks the girl straight in the eyes.

"I am no longer blind. I can see everything. I started getting my vision back awhile ago, but only now I can see clearly, like before being shot." FL bows his head.

"How do I look to you? Am I beautiful enough to be your woman?" the girl asks calmly.

"You are very beautiful. There is no one as beautiful as you."

The girl takes FL's hand in hers and kisses it.

"I am so happy you can see again, that you can see me. I have been waiting for this moment for a long time. Looking you in the eyes and telling you that I love you. Now that moment has come. Why didn't you tell me earlier that you can see?" she asks.

"I was afraid of your reaction. I thought maybe you would send me on my way or tell your brother," FL replies.

"I would have done this." The girl puts her arms around FL's neck and kisses him passionately on the mouth. They kiss and kiss and kiss some more. "Now let's go and start our new life together, my love." She grabs FL's hand and draws him toward the door. They pick up the luggage, take a good look at the apartment for the last time, and bolt out of there, down the stairs and out the front door. She doesn't even lock the door. She doesn't care anymore about that apartment and its contents. As far as she is concerned, that place is empty; there is nothing in there that she wants. She has everything she wants right in her hands.

They stop running when they hit the main street. Holding hands and each carrying a bag, they walk on the sidewalk looking straight ahead. Focused and in love. FL says, "We can go to a safe house belonging to an old friend of mine a few blocks from here. I have clothes and money stashed there. From there we get a car and go over to my other friend's place where I have hidden more money. Don't worry my love. My friends are not going to hurt you. Sorry for what happened to your brother but no harm will come your way. From there we go to a travel agency, book ourselves a vacation in Mexico, and get the hell out of Dodge."

They get to Panda's house after half an hour of walking on the main street and one of the side streets. They come to a blue house, an older home with a small veranda in the front. It looks and smells like it was freshly painted. A good-looking house. FL likes older homes; they have more character than the shit boxes they build today.

FL rings the front door bell. *Ringgggg, ringggggggggg*, more *ringggggggggg*. They hear movement in the house, and finally the front door opens. A large Japanese man opens the door, and as soon as he sees FL, he bows and says something in Japanese. FL bows back and introduces the girl to his friend. They both walk into the house, and Panda closes the door.

"Panda, so good to see you, my friend. I am here to pick up some clothes and money. Are they still where I left them?" FL asks Panda.

"Good to see you too, FL. It's been a while, my friend. I thought you were dead until I saw Jap and he told me you still alive. Yes, they are exactly where you left them. I didn't need them. The clothes don't fit me, and I have money," Panda says jokingly. Panda gives FL a big hug and looks toward the girl.

"You are not the type he usually goes for. Who are you?" Panda asks the girl as soon as FL disappears into the hallway.

"I am the sister of the cop who shot FL. I have been taking care of FL for all this time. FL and I are in love and are going to run away to Mexico together. Any more questions, fat boy?"

"I like you," Panda says with a big smile. "You are rough and tough. He needs that in a girl," Panda adds, again with a big smile on his face. "Come, my girl. I have just made some sake tea—sake and green tea. Really good for you, especially at this time of day." Panda directs the girl toward the living room.

The interior of the house is very Japanese. It's a sharp contrast to its exterior, which is like one of those houses you see in the old fairytale books. The interior is like a Japanese Shinto shrine. The artwork is just amazing. The girl has no idea whether they are originals. She doesn't dare to ask the question. The girl has always been fascinated by the Japanese culture and its people. She very much respects the Japanese for their honor and respect for one another. Japanese have immense respect for nature and their elders. Disciplined people who at the same time do crazy shit that no one else even dreams of.

The paintings are mainly of samurai heroes, with an odd painting of a geisha inside a tavern. There are also a couple of paintings of Japan's famous cherry blossoms in Kyoto. She recognizes a couple of the samurais in the paintings. One is Miyamoto Musashi, and the other Honda Tadakatsu. Miyamoto Musashi was a ronin samurai, one of the most celebrated and remembered. He was a magnificent swordsman. Honda Tadakatsu was a general and a warrior in the army of the Four Heavenly Kings of Tokugawa. The girl was in heaven, looking around this majestic home, its artwork, plants, and exquisite furniture.

FL returns with two bags, one smaller than the other. He looks at the girl and tells her the money is in the bigger bag. He also tells the girl he has a friend who can help him launder the money and divide it over three credit cards. All legitimate! They both thank Panda, and FL asks to borrow his car to go over to Jap's place; he will leave the car there. Panda, without asking any questions, hands over the keys to FL. FL and the girl say their good-byes to Panda and go out of the house through the back door. A pimped-up Acura is parked in the back. It is also blue, and all its windows are tinted. A cool winged spoiler in the back, and a big-ass exhaust pipe sticking from the bottom. The interior of the car is straight from the movies, all custom made. (My dear reader – share with me your custom made design favorites) FL opens the passenger door for the girl and runs to the other side of the car to the driver's seat.

"Fasten your seatbelt hon, this is going to be the ride of a lifetime," FL tells the girl and starts the engine.

Vroooooom vrooooooommmmm vrooooooommmmmmm. The car sounds so sexy. *Vrrrooooooommmmmmm.* The car backs into the alley, and FL puts it in gear and presses the gas pedal. The car jerks forward pushing the girl back in her seat. The girl wonders whether this car has a jet engine built into it, it has so much power.

"There is a custom-made V8 Acura engine in this beauty. It is *fast*. But we have to be careful not to attract any attention while driving this baby."

FL is a damn good driver. He corners and turns with barely any effort. He knows these streets very well, feels he could drive them with his eyes closed.

The girl finally says something. "Is this the type of car you stole?"

"Not really. I stole mostly Porsches and trucks. I may have stolen one Honda, but mostly Porsche and trucks. High-end trucks! We have friends in the ports around here. Good friends, if you know what I mean. I steal the cars, a group of people change the appearance of the vehicle, and then they are sent abroad. They're mostly sent to the Far East—to mainland China, Hong Kong, and Taiwan. We also had some clients in Russia, Ukraine, and Slovakia."

"How many cars had you stolen until that fateful day?" the girl asks, this time a bit more relaxed, without holding on to her seat belt for dear life.

"Funny you should ask. I have stolen so many, you might think I may not remember exactly how many. But I do remember every one of them. Interesting; no one has ever asked me this question until now. You have to know everything, right?" FL takes his eyes off the road for a split second and looks at the girl and smiles. "Not counting the fuck-up of the night that I got shot, eighty-eight."

"Eighty-eight! *God*! That's so many. Did it lose its thrill after a while?"

"No! It never lost its thrill. Every time I did it, it was exhilarating. A high that no drug can match. Your heart beats like you've just sprinted 400 meters. I just can't describe it, the adrenaline rush! My job as a stock broker is also exciting, but not exciting enough. Too many rules in trading stocks! I don't like too many rules. Nicking cars had no rules. Steal the car, drive as fast and as carefully as you can to your destination, modify the car, sell it, and collect the cash. Just talking about it is making me excited," FL tells the girl and moves his right hand over the girl's bare thighs and starts to stroke them. His right hand suddenly becomes a busy one, changing gears and stroking the upper thighs of the girl when not shifting. It's FL's favorite combination of right hand use. He slowly moves his hand further up, and he touches the edge of her panty. He pulls the panty to one side and ever so gently rubs the outer part of the girl's pussy with his fingers. It's already wet, and he hasn't even started.

"You are wet," FL tells the girl, like she doesn't know already.

"I got wet when you touched my thighs. Your touch makes me so wet." It feels so good." She smiles and leans her head back.

FL removes his hand and shifts gears. When they reach a long stretch of uninterrupted road, he puts his hand where he left off, this time putting his index finger inside the girl's pussy.

"Ahhhhhhhhhh, hmmmmmmm, that's it, baby. Keep it right there. Ahhhhhhhhh, ahhhhhhhh, ooohhhhhhhh, so good," she moans with a smile.

FL is drives while playing inside the girl's pussy, multitasking at its finest. His index and middle fingers are slightly inside her, and he reaches ever so deeper and moves both his index and middle fingers gently in a running motion. She is now moaning even louder and is twisting her body left and right and moving her hips up and down. She reaches climax outside Jap's estate gate.

At the mansion FL gets out of the car and rushes up the steps to the front door. After a few minutes the door opens, and an older gentleman in a black suit opens the door. FL and the man exchange pleasantries, and FL rushes back to the car.

"Let's go inside. Jap is waiting for us in the house. Panda called him and told him we are on the way," FL grabs the bags and while holding the girl's hand runs up the stairs and through the front door into the mansion.

"This place has twenty rooms and five full bathrooms. We're going to stay here until I can get the money laundered and obtain passports," FL tells the girl. "We will be safe here."

The girl is looking around the mansion; there is more Japanese artwork here but not as congested as the last place. Panda's place was much smaller, and there was so much stuff. Here everything is well spaced. There are also artworks from well-known non-Japanese artists, and some of them look authentic. *So much wealth in this house*, she thinks.

FL can tell exactly what is going through her head and tells her that most of the artwork was purchased by Jap's father, who was once partner in many different businesses in Japan. Jap's father passed away a couple of years ago and left everything to Jap, an only child. His mother left the family and ran away with an American when Jap was only two. Jap has no idea what happened to his mother, and he doesn't even care. He helps FL with modifying cars in his private garage at the back of the estate. Jap has a butler, who opened the door, a couple of maids, and two cooks. He also has many girls living in the mansion with him.

"So don't be surprised if you see many women in lingerie or even sometimes naked running around the house. Jap loves women, good food, and fast cars," FL tells the girl while they walk to the main room, where Jap is waiting for them. Jap greets FL with a bow and then a bear hug. Jap is the complete opposite of Panda. He is slim, with long hair, and very well dressed. He is wearing a dark grey suit with white stripes. Under the suite he is wearing a very shiny pink dress shirt, together with a gray-and-pink patterned tie. *Very good-looking man*, the girl thinks. In the room are also two girls in lingerie, preparing drinks for Jap and his guests.

"Hello, there. Pleased to meet you." Jap extends his hand to the girl, and they shake.

"Welcome to my home. Please sit down and make yourself comfortable. My home is your home." He gestures to the girl. "FL is like a brother to me, and his woman like a sister."

The girl settles on one of the many sofas in the room, curls her legs up, and tucks them underneath her. The butler brings her a drink and a snack.

"I hope this will do until dinner, madam," the butler tells the girl in a melodious French accent. "Dinner will be served in couple of hours." He hands the girl her drink and a plate with her snack. The snack consists of a turkey breast sandwich in a Kaiser bun with a Caesar salad.

"Thank you. It looks delicious." The girl smiles at the butler and puts the drink and the large plate on the side table next to the sofa.

She looks around but doesn't see FL and Jap. They have disappeared somewhere in this mansion. Her mind wanders to her brother. She wonders how he is doing and if he has found out about their disappearance. It has been close to twenty-four hours since they left her apartment.

Constable Johnson is doing everything in his power to leave the hospital and go over to his sister's place. The doctors will not have it. He is to remain in hospital for at least two more days so they can monitor his progress and see if he needs any surgery on his hand. Johnson assures them that he is all right and can go back to work, but the hospital staff would have none of that bullshit, and they made sure there was a full-time monitor so he would not leave the hospital without proper discharge. Johnson lies in the hospital bed wondering how long he is going to be stuck there. Now he understands how FL must have felt, lying on that bed. He hasn't been there for more than a couple of hours, and he is sick of it already. He never had to be hospitalized before in his life. He despises hospitals. He has tubes coming out of his arm, and his hand is bandaged very well. He is not feeling any pain, but he knows why; it's because he is pumped up with morphine. *Now, that's what morphine feels like. No wonder people get addicted to it. It is a pretty good feeling.*

His friend walks into his room and comes over and asks him how he is doing.

"I'm doing better with this morphine going through me. Now I know how it feels on this stuff. No wonder more and more people are getting hooked on this shit."

"Look, buddy. I asked around the neighborhood, and your story doesn't match what some of the eyewitnesses are telling me. You told me that they were kids, and a couple of people who saw the whole thing tell me different." Johnson's friend speaks quietly, so only he and Johnson can hear, even though there is no one else in the room.

"What do these witnesses tell you?" Johnson asks.

"You tell me, buddy. Who are you protecting here? You can tell me, my friend. I am here to help you. Please tell me who really attacked you."

"You tell me what the witnesses tell you, and I will tell you my story." Johnson is not giving in.

"Okay, I know you. You will not tell me anything until I tell you what you want to hear. The witnesses told me there were two male adults, one Asian and the other maybe Middle Eastern. When you went to your cruiser, they approached you from the back, and you did not turn around. Both witnesses say that after a few minutes you grabbed your hand and went down, and the two men moved away from you in the opposite direction, very fast. That's when the crowd of people came to your aid. Who were those two men? What did they want with you?"

"Okay. I will tell you. They were friends of FL, and they wanted some kind of revenge on me for killing him. They knew I killed him and disposed of his body. They are not killers, so they didn't kill me. All they wanted to do was to hurt me."

"You disposed of the dude's body? Why did you do that? That's not legal, my friend. There should have been an autopsy. I'm not going to say anything, but, man, if anyone finds out, you are in big shit." The cop has a mixture of surprise and disgust on his face. "The report you filed said that you shot and killed him, and you didn't have your radio on, and you went back to your car to call for an ambulance, and when you went back to his body, it was no longer there."

"I lied on the report, buddy. I disposed of the body. I didn't want any trace of him anywhere. I didn't want to answer any questions regarding how it all went down. I have been chasing this son of a bitch for so many years! I finally got him, and by disposing of his body I closed that chapter forever. I know what I did is very wrong and way against the rules, but what is done is done, and I can't go back and change anything. You have a choice, and I will not hold it against you if you report this. You are first a cop and then my friend. I leave it to you to decide." Johnson closes his eyes. "I'm going to get some rest now, my friend. I had a bad day and need to be alone now."

"Okay, buddy. I will come and visit you tomorrow. You take it easy. One scumbag off the streets is better than one on them. I understand, so rest assured that your secret is safe with me forever. I'm your friend first and then a cop," Johnson's friend tells him before he leaves the room. Johnson is relieved that he could make up that story on the fly and that his friend bought it. It seems both him and FL are off the hook. Everyone thinks the guy is dead. He doesn't need to go back to his sister's apartment and see if he is still there. Johnson is sure that FL, with his connections, can easily change his identification and live a different life with his sister, perhaps even away from here. He cannot afford to be seen around town anymore. He is supposed to be dead, for God's sake.

Johnson feels now he has a clear conscience about the whole ordeal with FL. Yes, he lied to his friend, but he had to in order to protect himself and his sister. He also wanted to protect his arch nemesis, FL. When Johnson last visited his sister's apartment, he could feel the love the two had for each other. They had fallen in love, and he wasn't about to break that love. True love is too precious to be deliberately destroyed. If his sister and FL were not in love, then he would give that son of a bitch up, but for the sake of his sister, he just couldn't let himself do that. Johnson loved her too much. She was the only family member he had left. He hopes that one day he would hear from her again, but he knows that it will not be for a long while. Johnson goes into a dream, and it's a damn good one.

FL and the girl leave Jap's place after a week of wine-and-dine. They have been treated like royalty, and in such a way they don't want to leave. They have it so good. Jap insists that they can stay, but FL and the girl are adamant that it's a big risk for them all. All the paperwork is in place. They have new passports with new identities. They are Randy and Jillian Smith. They buy their tickets to Mexico City, and Jap gives them the address of a fellow Japanese businessman who will hook them up with money and a place to stay anywhere they choose to live in Mexico. Jap drives them to the airport. There, Jap only bows; this time and does not hug either of them. FL and the girl bow back and thank him for all his help. FL has kept the thick moustache and beard. The girl has cut her hair short and has also colored it. They look like any ordinary innocent lovebirds that are travelling together. They check in and go through airport security with no problems. They board the flight and sit next to each other in silence until the plane doors are closed and the pilot comes on the speaker welcoming the passengers. FL is anxious to leave the city and his old life behind. He is restless and squeezing the girl's hand very hard.

"It's going to be okay. Don't be so nervous. We're going to take off very soon. Once that happens, we are free, my love. Just the two of us," the girl calmly says to FL and kisses his cheek.

"Mr. and Mrs. Smith?" A flight attendant interrupts the lovebirds.

"Yes. Is there anything wrong?" FL asks nervously. He is now pressing the girl's hand so hard she has to pull it out of his.

"There is a phone call for you from a Constable Johnson. He has told us not to leave the gate until he speaks to you, sir," the flight attendant tells FL. "Please follow me to the back." FL unfastens his seat belt and, nervously glancing at the girl, gets up and follows the flight attendant.

"Hello. This is Randy Smith. May I ask what this is all about?" FL says on the phone. His voice is so low as to be barely audible. His voice is also cracking from nerves.

"Hello, Mr. Smith. This is Constable Johnson. I'm not sure if my sister ever told you about me, but I'm Jillian's older brother. We have been apart for many years, and recently I found out she has married and is on her way to Mexico. I just wanted to wish you and her all the best. Please tell her I'm well and will expect a phone call from her when you guys get to Mexico. Okay?" Johnson very calmly says.

"Oh no, she didn't tell me about you, Constable Johnson. I appreciate your call, sir. I will surely give her your message. Does she have your number?" FL replies, now somewhat calmer.

"Yes, she does have the number. I wish you both all the best. Are you going to be staying in Mexico for awhile, son?" Johnson asks.

"We don't know, sir. We might."

"The longer, the better, son. Then I can come and visit," Johnson tells FL.

"I look forward to meeting you one day, sir. Thank you, and have a lovely day," FL replies with a smile.

"Take care of my sister, son. Good-bye." Johnson doesn't wait for a reply and hangs up the phone.

FL returns to his seat and sees that the girl has been crying. He wasn't sure why she was crying. Did she think they were in trouble? Was she missing her brother?

"How did it go?" the girl asks.

"He wished us well and told me to stay away as long as we could and that he would come and visit us. And, oh, he told me to tell you to call him when you get there," FL replies.

"Really? So no problems! No trouble for us! I can't believe he did this. I was afraid cops were going to storm the plane and take both of us away in handcuffs." The girl bursts into tears and starts to laugh at the same time. Tears of joy this time!

"Your brother is an amazing man, my love. He didn't let me die in a dirty alleyway, had his sister takes care of me, and now is letting me go to live a new life with you. He has sacrificed everything for me. I can't imagine what he is going through right now. I know he loves and cares for you more than anything in this world, and it is because of this love for you that he has set both of us free. He is a bigger man than I could ever be. I just can't figure out how he knew our names and the flight we were on." FL replies.

"Well, when I went to the bathroom in the terminal before boarding the plane I called him and told him we are travelling on this flight to Mexico city under these names. I wanted to hear his voice and say goodbye. When the flight attendant came by and told you he was on the phone and wanted to talk to you I regretted what I had done. I didn't know what he was going to say to you or do. I am just glad I didn't screw it up for us. I am sorry my love. I miss him very much."

"It is fine my dear. It worked out for the best. We both had a chance to talk to him and I am glad it happened."

The pilot's voice comes on the speaker. "Cabin crew; please get ready for takeoff."

The Airbus comes to a halt at the start of the runway, the engines start to roar, and the big plane rushes forward with a remarkable thrust. After a few minutes, the plane is up in the air, and the city in which FL lived for so many years is now below him. How small everything is from up here! He looks down and sees minicars traveling the streets. The same streets he maneuvered when he had stolen a car. The same streets he ran from Johnson and his colleagues. The same streets that brought him down, which then led him to this beautiful person.

"I love you, Mrs. Smith," FL tells the girl.

"I love you, Mr. Smith," the girl replies, and they both look out of the plane window down to the city that they cannot come back to for a long, long time or perhaps forever.

"I promised your brother that I will take care of you. I will be by your side until the day I die, my love," FL tells the girl.

"Well, what goes around comes around, right? I took care of you, and now I guess it's your turn, baby. … I am just joking, my love. We will take care of each other. That's how two people who love each other live. I take a load off your shoulders, and you do the same for me." The girl says this with a smile that could light up the whole plane.

FL and the girl stay in Mexico City for three months, then move from one town to another, until finally settling in a small fishing village in Baja California. They buy a small home in a cute village near La Paz, and FL buys a fishing boat and starts to run a fishing charter. The girl starts a small school for teaching English, and before long she has many students. The fees she charges are minimal, so the locals can afford to come. FL and the girl run their respective businesses during the day, and their nights are spent on the beach that fronts their home, with their neighbors and neighbors' friends and families. They don't have any guests of their own, since they have not told anyone of their whereabouts, not even Johnson. The girl called Johnson when they arrived in Mexico City and told him that once they were settled, she would contact him again. It took her four more months before he called her brother again.

"Hello. This is Constable Johnson. Can I help you?" Johnson's serious voice comes on the line.

"Hello, my dear brother. How are you?" the girl's voice comes on the other end of the line.

"Oh, my darling sister, I am so glad to hear from you again. It has been so long. God, I miss you so much, my dear. How are you? How is FL? I am good, my dear. Same old, same old. Running after criminals."

"FL is now officially my husband, my dear brother. We got married a month ago on the beach by a village elder that has authority to marry people here."

"My dear, congratulations! You have made me so happy. Wow, you made my day. Such great news!"

"Another good news, my good brother: I am also three months pregnant. The baby is due at Christmas, and we would love for you to come and join us for that."

"I'm going to be an uncle this Christmas? This is the best day of my life!" Johnson starts singing "What a Wonderful World" by Louis Armstrong.

"Yes, you are going to be the best uncle in the world," the girl replies. "Please tell me you will come. FL runs a fishing charter boat, and you both can go together on the boat fishing and just relax, my good brother. You need this time off. Please tell me you are coming. I miss you so much." The girl bursts into tears.

"I miss you too, my darling sister. There's not a day that goes by that I don't think about you and what you are doing. You are in my thoughts every day." Johnson sobs too and tries to collect himself.

"Fishing, eh? Sounds like FL found himself a good gig down there. Anyway, where are you in the world that he is running a fishing charter?"

"We're in a small village just south of La Paz in Baja California. You can fly into Cabo, and we'll pick you up there."

"Done! I will take the whole month of December off and come down there," Johnson replies excitedly.

"Now you've made me the happiest girl in the world, my dear brother. Please tell us your flight information when you book it, and we will be at the airport to pick you up."

"I can't wait to see you guys. Have a wonderful day, my dear. Love you."

"Love you too. See you soon," the girl replies and hangs up the phone.

That night when FL returns from work, she tells him about the phone call and how she convinced Johnson to come for a visit, as they had discussed the night before. FL is happy about the news. He wants the opportunity to tell Johnson face-to-face how much he appreciates what he has done for him. He wants to make it up to Johnson.

"It's so funny, my dear. Your brother shot and nearly killed me, but I'm looking forward to seeing him and thanking him for doing that. If he hadn't done what he did, I would have never met you and would still be living the life of a car thief and a stock broker, which is also stealing people's money in a way. I would have remained a thief for my whole life. I am so much happier living a simple life in this beautiful paradise with you and our little family." FL gives his wife a big hug and rubs her tummy.

"I'm glad you look at it this way. Any other person would go through life holding a grudge against that person."

"Well, that other person would have never met you, so I can understand why he would hold a grudge." FL laughs and takes his wife's hand.

Constable Johnson cannot share his excitement with anyone. He has told whoever knew his sister or of his sister that she went to South America, exactly where he doesn't say. She was tired of the city and wanted a simpler life. She calls him once in a while, they chat, and that's it. He requests the whole month of December off, and his superiors do not even flinch. They all agree that he deserves a holiday.

"I bought my ticket, my dear sister!" he announces as soon as someone answers his call.

"Hi. This is not your sister. This is FL. Do I sound like her?" FL replies with a smile.

"Oh no, sorry. You don't. I just said what was on my mind, assuming she would pick up the phone," Johnson replies, embarrassed.

"It's okay, brother. I had the day off today. Taking the missus to the hospital in La Paz for her regular checkup. She's at the local market right now. Once she's back, we're going to La Paz. Her doctor is very good. Very caring doctors here!"

"I just wanted to let you guys know I booked my flight and will be there December 1. I won't be coming back here until after the new year, so expect me to stay with you guys for a while," Johnson tells FL with great excitement. "This is my first real holiday. Now that I don't have to chase you anymore, I can take time off," Johnson laughs.

"You are very welcome. We have an extra room in the house just for you," FL replies. "I am a good boy here, brother. I go to work every day and take rich people fishing. I used to be one of those rich guys, but I'm much happier this way. I'm not as rich in the pocketbook as I used to be, but my soul is richer with love and kindness. I am so content, and I could not be any happier."

"That is the key word, my friend: content! Being content these days doesn't exist, since we just want more and more, but one day it has to stop, and you must be happy with who you are and what you have." Johnson presses a button on the phone.

"Got you on the speaker phone now, my friend. My dinner is about to boil over. Need to get it off the stove!" Johnson shouts.

"Well, my savior, go and eat your dinner. I will tell my darling wife you called with the good news. Please take care until then, and don't get shot!" FL replies and laughs again.

"And don't shoot anyone." Johnson laughs too.

"Good-bye," FL calls.

"Thank you for everything, FL. You are also mine and my sister's savior. This whole thing was a win-win situation, and I could not have planned it any better. Good-bye."

The baby boy is born on the fourth day of Johnson's visit. It is a long and painful labor for the girl, but she is strong and manages well without any drugs. The baby boy is a big one, with lots of hair. They name the baby boy after FL's favorite person on earth, John Lennon. John is close to nine pounds and has FL's chin and eyes. Proud daddy is holding John in his arms while Johnson is talking to his sister at her bedside.

"He is so beautiful, my dear. He is a beautiful blend of both you guys," Johnson tells his sister while holding her hand in his. She is a bit weak, and she manages to smile back at him before closing her eyes. She is very tired but also very proud to give FL a son to carry his name. FL didn't really care about the kid's gender as long as the kid was healthy at birth. FL had already told his wife that he wanted five children, and she didn't even blink at the idea of going through pregnancy and labor four more times. She wanted to give FL anything he wanted that was in her power to give.

"One down and four more to go," FL tells his sleepy wife while holding the baby in his arms. The baby is quiet, and his eyes are closed, but his arms and legs are moving.

"Bring him over to me. I want to look at him again," FL's wife requests in a faint voice. FL brings the baby over and hands him to his mother. She starts stroking his hair ever so gently and brings him to her nose so she can smell him. He smells so innocent! All babies have that beautiful scent, the aroma of innocence. When is innocence lost? At what age? Two, three, four, ten? *I lost mine when I was six*, FL thinks to himself. He lost his innocence when a female teacher in his school fondled him after class. He remembers her being very pretty and tall, and him just standing there while she was touching him in all the wrong places.

"Let's go, my brother, and leave her and little John alone. She needs all the rest she can get," FL tells Johnson.

"Where are we going?" Johnson asks.

"We're taking the boat out into the sea, and then we're going to park it somewhere in the open sea and have a drink and smoke a big fat cigar," FL replies and walks over to his wife and little boy.

"Have a good rest, my love. See you tomorrow. I hope we can all go home tomorrow." FL kisses her forehead and little Johnny's hand and leaves the room. Johnson grabs his sister's hand and kisses it and follows FL out of the room into the hospital corridor. The hospital in La Paz is a brand-new state-of-the-art facility, and everyone working there has been so nice to FL and his wife.

FL and Johnson drive FL's Jeep toward the docks where FL's boat is moored. They get to the boat around two in the morning. It takes FL just ten minutes to get it out of the little marina, and they are off into the Sea of Cortez. There is a bright half-moon shining down into the water, and they can see billions of stars scattered across the night sky, some shining brighter than others.

Johnson breaks the silence. "We don't get to see this in the city."

"Yes. I never get tired of looking at this. It is endless and beautiful," FL replies.

"So, you think the universe is endless?"

"Well, to date we have not found where the universe begins or ends, right? So, based on the facts today, I believe it is endless."

"So you are not a religious man. You don't believe that the universe was created by God in so many days and that he planted the animals and then humans?"

"No, my friend. I don't believe any of that mumbo jumbo. Here, have a *cerveza*." FL hands Johnson a bottle of Sole beer. "This is my favorite beer here."

"Funny. This is also my favorite beer," Johnson tells FL.

"I really hope one day before I die I can go up in space and look down at Mother Earth. From space there are no manmade border lines and territories. The only border lines are where land meets water. No countries and no religion too!" FL jumps into the famous song by John Lennon "Imagine." This song is his favorite. He knows every word, and he doesn't have a bad voice either.

"Imagine there is no heaven, it's easy if you try, no hell below us, above us only sky, imagine all the people living for today." FL sings and takes a sip of his Sole beer and steers his Bayliner fishing boat farther out into the open waters. The sea is very calm, and there is hardly any wind, which makes their little boat trip even better. FL lights up a cigar and hand it over to Johnson and lights one more up for himself and starts puffing.

"That night when you shot me and then found me in the alleyway, what was going through your mind?" FL suddenly asks.

"The thought was "I got you!" Finally I got you, but that was not the way I wanted to get you. I wanted to arrest you and take you in. I had no intention of shooting you. I don't like using my gun. The gun is for my protection and not for aggression. But when you came out shooting, I had no other choice, and a couple of my bullets got to you. When I saw you bleeding in that filthy alleyway, I decided that's not the way for you to go down. Not the great FL. So I did what I did, and the rest you know. My initial plan was for you to get a bit better and then take you in. Tell them that you gave yourself up after being wounded in the shootout. But you were not well for a long time, so I just stuck to my story that I saw you in the alleyway dead, and when I returned back to your location your body was gone. I told the cops that you had many friends in the area, and that they must have taken your body away. I had to lie in order to protect myself, my sister, and also you."

"Then how did I end up being blind for awhile after I finally came out of unconsciousness?" FL asked.

"That's a mystery to me too. I have no idea how you were blinded and then got your sight back. Maybe it had to do with you being in a state of bliss for that long or the bullet which passes through your face. I am glad you can see again, though." Johnson gets up from his seat and walks back toward FL.

"Can I drive the boat for a bit?"

"Of course you can. Here, crank it if you like." FL hands the wheel over to Johnson.

"No need to go faster than this. This is just the perfect speed, FL," Johnson tells FL and takes over the wheel.

The boat bops around in the water while moving forward at a steady pace, and Johnson is enjoying driving it. In the open waters with no one around, one can drive the boat with eyes closed. There is nothing in the water to watch out for, and you are not going to get blindsided by an idiot driver.

"I can really can get used to this kind of living, you know," Johnson says.

"Then, why don't you? You are always welcome to stay here with us, and I can use someone I can trust to help me out with the business. If I get one more boat, we make serious money. My clients love me, and they refer me to their friends, but I only have one boat and it's just me. If you come on board, then I can spend more time with my wife and kid also."

"Last year I was in the streets looking for you, to catch you and take you off the streets. I would have never thought a year will change so many things that you and I became friends, family and maybe partners," Johnson replies with a big smile.

"Well, you did catch me and take me off the streets. So you achieved what you set out to do. Your main goal was for me to not steal cars anymore, and you can see I am no longer in the stealing nice cars business. I am a changed man, thanks to you. You and your sister transformed me. I am a better and, more importantly, content person. I never could achieve that without the circumstances that led me to be here with you and her and, now, my little boy." FL takes a sip from his beer and looks out at the wide open sea.

"So, are you serious about becoming partners? I need to go back and sell my assets and bring the money here. It would take a while for me to do that. Is that going to be okay with you?" Johnson asks. He is totally excited with this proposal from FL. This can be his ticket out of the craziness of his life.

"Surely, do what needs to be done and come here, my brother. You will not want to go back," FL replies. He is also excited about the idea of being partners with his love's brother, his brother-in-law. He can now call him that since he is legally married to Johnson's sister. And the irony of it: a year ago FL hated this man, and now he is married to his sister and offering to be partners with him. How life changes course without any warning, and in his case for the better. They both feel the excitement the same way, in their guts. The excitement is deep in their guts, rushing upward with so much force it makes them sick. Sick in a good way. Johnson had felt like this when he was chasing FL and knowing he was about to get him. FL felt like this every time he stole a car. However, this feeling is way more intense than the others. It is much deeper in the gut. This is the truest form of gut feeling.

Johnson stays another couple of weeks with FL, his sister and little John. Upon his return, Johnson turns in his notice of resignation on his first day back in the office. He tells his colleagues that he has had enough of this lifestyle and needed a simpler and a more stress-free life. He is moving down to Baja California and will run a fishing charter with a friend he met down there. He invites all his colleagues to come and visit him down there, and he will give them a good discount on fishing. The next thing he does is put his condo up for sale. One of his colleagues was married to a good real estate agent, and he hires her to sell his condo. He sells his household belongings, packs a couple of suitcases, sends one to his sister's address in Baja, and takes the other case and leaves town.

He travels to Toronto and Montreal to watch a couple of his favorite hockey teams in action before heading down to his final destination of Baja California. He is really going to miss hockey.

The thought of not being able to go to a game once in a while to watch the action live or on TV when he has the chance bothers him.

The apartment sells in two months, for more than his asking price. The guy who buys it is one of the junior detectives whose wife had come into a nice inheritance. Johnson is his hero. He wants to live in the same apartment as his all-time idol and mentor. So he makes Johnson an offer he cannot refuse. After traveling to Ontario, Quebec, and the Maritimes, Johnson is ready to part with his beloved Canada.

"I will see you again, my love. I will come up and visit, since you can't come down. I will love you till the day I die, my love," Johnson tells Canada and boards his flight to Cabo San Lucas from Vancouver.

At the airport FL and the girl are waiting for Johnson. The child is at the neighbors. They all embrace for a long time, just embracing each other and not letting go, without saying a word. Just holding! They feel each other's souls floating through them and embracing as well. Amazing feeling. They feel as if they are lifted to the airport's roof, hovering over everybody in that embraced position. They don't want to let go. The moment has arrived that the two enemies have come together embracing in the name of love.

On the way home FL tells Johnson that he has set up a high-tech satellite system with all the channels. They can watch hockey together and have hockey game parties with the neighbors.

It cannot get any better than this, Johnson tells himself. If there is a heaven in the afterworld, I want it to be just like this forever.

Johnson and FL both had different priorities in their lives, with their greed controlling them, and them not controlling it. FL was obsessed with making more money to have more chicks and have more money to have even more chicks. Johnson's obsession was to use anything to catch FL and lock him up. He didn't care for anything else in life as much, not even himself or his beloved sister. Once he caught FL, he felt like *Now what? I obsessed my whole life over this one person, and now he is there dying. I can't let this happen.* He saved FL's life to satisfy his own greed. He couldn't let go. He couldn't close the chapter. Not like that, anyway. Their uncontrollable greed drove them to each other, and their love for a woman brought their greed under control and brought them together.

Johnson and FL continued running their successful fishing charter together for many years with only two boats. Johnson finally got married and started a family of his own after couple of years of being there. He fell in love with a local lady in the village. They were an item from his second week in Mexico. They got married on the beach by a village elder, just like FL and the girl.

Story 3

Mr. Ahmadi, Mr. Bandar, and Little Homa

Sounds of footsteps. Why they are called footsteps, I am not sure. They should really be called shoe steps. A foot does not make a sound. It is the shoe that one hears. Especially ladies' shoes. She is walking under my window. Sounds like she is wearing a fine pair of stiletto shoes. She is also taking nice steps. Firm and confident steps. Neither hurried nor lazily dragging along the ground. She lifts her foot up and brings it down in one slow motion. I wonder what she looks like. She may be a dancer. Dancers walk beautifully. Their walks have rhythm. Rhythmical steps. She walked gracefully when she wore high heels. She had pretty ankles. Full and muscular. How I miss her, and how I don't.

The woman stops walking, and now I hear her talking to a couple of men, giving them directions to a coffee shop. I had heard the two men walking up and down the street talking to one another prior to talking to her. They sure were looking for a place. This time they stop under my window having a heated discussion. From their tone I can pick up that they are seniors, and from their accent I gather that they are my fellow countrymen. However, they are speaking in English to each other. I hear a little girl talking from time to time to either of them. But they continue talking to each other.

Ahmadi: "Did you see that game? Ah, my God. Did you see how Iran played against Mexico? It brings tears into my heart to see them lose like that. I cannot believe it. Shame on them! Shame on that useless coach! First half they played beautifully, scored a goal—and the second half? My God, thinking about it makes me angry."

They speak in English because of their granddaughter, Homa, who does not understand Farsi very well but likes to know everything her grandfathers are saying. She is very fascinated by her granddads, most of all by their passion! She sees passion in everything they do. Passion even when they play cards with each other. They get most passionate when they talk about their pasts and how they remember their homeland. They both remember Iran fondly. They talk about Iran's beauty and its strengths. They also talk about its weakness and malice. They share their enjoyment of going to one of those many roadside restaurants high up in the mountains on their way to the Caspian Sea. Their shared enjoyment of eating kebabs with bread and yogurt and then having a nice nap by the river on a raised-up bed listening to the rush of the water going by. Sleeping and breathing in the fresh air blown in by a breeze that also cooled them down. These were their collective fondest memories. When they talked about jubilant events, they would talk with such joy. They really missed their lives in Iran, the simplicity of their lives and their outings. Nothing flashy or expensive or outrageous! No, just a simple act of eating in a roadside restaurant and then taking a nap before heading to the sea had all the enjoyment of the world in it for them. Pure love of life! In those days, Bandar and Ahmadi were part of a growing middle class in Iran, with hundreds of their fellow countrymen and countrywomen joining that rank every day.

Most of the time, with perhaps very few exceptions, the middle class of any society consists of its intellectuals, a group of people made up of subgroups such as teachers, nurses, doctors, musicians, writers, professors, merchants, journalists, middle and upper management, mechanics, plumbers, electricians, junior engineers, and architects, to name just a few. Different people with different backgrounds, lifestyles, and ambitions but equal in stature within their chosen society! They all share a common bond. They are all middle class; upper, middle, or lower middle is not an issue. Bourgeoisie! The ones who are the core of making up a powerful democratic society!

The middle class is usually mistaken for the masses. What good are the masses when they are not doing so well intellectually and financially? It's the middle class, the happy class, that carries the burdens and beauties of its society on its bare shoulders and creates opportunities and takes risks. The middle class sees and deals with the good, the bad, and the ugly of its society. This powerful phenomenon, which many progressive countries in this world enjoy, was beginning to take shape in Iran: the middle class movement!

The Islamic revolution in Iran put a halt to the middle class movement. The middle class is a danger to the fundamentalist ideology of an Islamic state. Bandar and Ahmadi were enjoying their middle-class lifestyles. Ahmadi's mom was a prominent university professor in prestigious Aryamehr Industrial University. She taught calculus. Her sister was partner in a law firm in Isfahan. Bandar's wife and sister were both high school teachers, teaching boys and girls in Bandar Abbas. Women and men worked side by side, building a strong country together. This was cut overnight with the arrival of Khomeini in Iran.

Another thing the Islamic revolution in Iran didn't like was the governments that had ties with Israel. They cursed and condemned the USA, the United Kingdom, France, and above all Israel for their atrocities around the world and especially their treatment of minorities and, in the case of Israel, Palestinian people. The Islamic regime in Iran condemned the same governments that brought it to power in the first place and has continued to keep in power to date. Why do I say this? Lets take a minute to think about this simple fact that where would the world of arms market be without the Israeli/Arab conflict? Nowhere! Israel against Arab war (in general all Moslems around the world) is the best pool of spiral conflict that fuels the arms market and keeps the arms making factories running at full speed. Now where and how will the money be generated when there is peace? How many doves and flowers one can sell to make as much money compared to selling arms? Only bullets, bombs and missiles turn billion dollar profits and not doves and flowers.

So now what can be added to this great pot of mayhem so it can continue to fuel this fantastic money making machine so it can be sustained for a long long time? Hmmmmmm lets see! Where can we fuck shit up so we can sell more arms and have gigantic budgets for Research and Development from its aftermath?" Questions asked by the Big Bosses but they already knew the answers. The Shah of Iran was gaining too much power and he was becoming a big pain in their royal asses like his father had become before he was exiled by the British. So we better get rid of this tyrant, murderous Shah Mohammad Reza Pahlavi of Iran. Lets get rid of him and establish a monster, so it will feed us forever. The Islamic Republic in Iran was, is, and will be that monster for many years to come. Many Iranian who are portrayed as monsters due to profitability of some no good cold blooded bastards, are sick to their stomachs and at this moment that's all they can be. Just be sick and disgusted with what is going on. There is not really anything anybody can do when Big Money is involved. They crush you like a little bug. Well, Big Money, screw you and your damn policies. I want to see you come and crush me.

Mr. Bandar: "Don't worry about it, Ahmadi. What is wrong with you? It is only a game. Why you take it so seriously? What are you going to get by them winning, hah?"

Mr. Ahmadi: "Pride. Bragging rights, okay. I hoped for our team to do well this World Cup. But I don't know what happened. In the second half, they just stopped playing. You saw that! How can you be so calm? Aren't you angry?"

Mr. Bandar: "I am, but what can we do? What is done is done. They lost. They were horrible, as always, and they lost. Plus, I hear rumors that the captain and couple of players got into a shouting match at halftime because one of the players was signing autographs for young girls. I don't know. Some rubbish like that."

Mr. Ahmadi: "If that is the case, then they deserve to lose. Those idiots! Ahmaghha, nafahmhaye bishoor! Stupid idiots! Ah, I am so mad now. Fight amongst themselves in their first game? How stupid and childlike. You know what I think. I think the government in Iran told them if you win this game, we will hurt you and your families. Can you imagine the streets of Tehran if Iran had beaten Mexico? It would have been celebrations everywhere, and those bisharfa [ones with no soul] over there don't want celebrations. That is what I think. Who cares, baba? Let's go and have some coffee around the corner. Good Italian coffee shops around here."

Bandar: "Italian coffee shops? Around here? Hahahahhahahahaha, you must be kidding! I don't think so, my friend. We are in Chinatown, not Commercial Drive. All along, you thought we are on the Drive. And here I am wondering why you are coming to this side of town. Commercial is on the other side."

Ahmadi: "Commercial, Chinatown—so? There must be a coffee place that sells authentic coffee somewhere around here. Why there are no coffee shops in Chinatown? The lady told us go around the corner and there is a coffee shop."

Bandar: "There are. Not authentic, though like the ones on Commercial Drive: Starbucks. Let's go. It is this way. I can't believe you thought we are by the Drive. Oh my God, come this way. Okay, so how is the family?"

The voices fade away, and no longer can I understand what they are saying. More white noise. I look at the ceiling and laugh at the last conversation I heard under my window. That guy was not happy. God, why can't I sleep? Tomorrow I have to deal with so much shit. I miss her so, and so I don't!

Mr. Bandar was a prominent businessman in the southern Iranian port city of Bandar Abbas before the Islamic revolution in Iran. He started in the city bazaar selling *hoboobat* (grains) in bulk through his own chamber. He was twelve when he first started in his uncle's chamber in the bazaar. While working during the day, he attended night school in another town two hours away, every night, so he could learn how to read and write. Mr. Bandar was a natural in mathematics. Had he continued his schooling after grade school, he would have become a prominent mathematician. With only grade school under his belt, he knew more math than many college students he met. Since he was very good with numbers, he ran a profitable business for his uncle. By the time he was sixteen, his uncle made him a partner in the business, and they opened up a second chamber in Khoramshahr, another city in southern Iran, very close to Kuwait and Iraq. The city of Khoramshahr was very much destroyed during the senseless Iran/Iraq war.

Bandar was a brilliant businessman, and by the age of twenty he was one of the most prominent grain wholesalers in Iran, servicing many retail shops in major cities in Iran, plus most of the neighboring Gulf countries.

His great personality and fair way of conducting business caused the farmers to love him and want to deal with him exclusively. Many wholesalers abused the farmers, since they were not really protected by the government or any other agency. The farmers lived in villages without electricity and proper fresh running water and sewer systems. They did not own their lands, and they worked mostly to pay off the landlords, with very little money left for them and their families. Mr. Bandar looked after his farmer suppliers. Mr. Bandar dealt solely with local farmers in his province and a handful of other ones in southern provinces. The business was thriving, and the entire Bandar clan was benefiting from this success.

During the shah's time, the business tax was not really enforced. Most of the money for running the government came from the sale of oil and other natural resources, which Iran had and has plenty of. The businessmen like Bandar kept most of the money after paying off their expenses and very little tax, nothing close to what they should have been paying. Most bazaar merchants in Iran did not pay even that small amount for taxes during the shah's regime. Most claimed that they follow the Islamic way of giving through Khoms and Zakat, which really didn't help out the government. One doesn't give one's government money willingly. One would rather give to the poor, the needy, and the old than to the government.

No one believed in giving to the government. They saw the lavish lives of the government officials and rightly told them to go fuck themselves when they came around collecting taxes. "Don't tell me you need to tax me when I see how you live. You don't need my money. You already have enough. No! Spend less on yourselves, and I may consider giving you some more money, but not until then. Right now it's one big fat *no*!" That was the message from the bazaar businesses all over Iran.

Mr. Bandar did not give any Khoms or Zakat either, since he was not religious. He didn't believe in Islam. He felt really out of place in the bazaar during the holy month of Ramadan and other Shiite religious rituals. Except for Bandar and a couple of others who had to pretend to be religious, the rest were truly devoted Shiite Muslims. Bandar had to go with the flow and pretend and lie; otherwise, they would have run him out of the bazaar in minutes. So every Eid Ghorban (Eid Al-Adha), he would kill a sheep and distribute the meat and pretend he gave Khoms and Zakat. He went to Mecca for pilgrimage with a few of his clients in the Middle East. He did not find the experience a holy one. He enjoyed the historical aspects of the pilgrimage rather than the religious.

Years earlier, planning and executing the trip in secret, he went to Thailand. There he learned about the teachings of Buddha. He found Buddhist traditions and rituals intriguing and making more sense than the teachings of Islam. He respected the simplicity of life within the Buddhist religion and Buddha's teachings of peace, self-respect, and healing. The Western religions promote the blame game rather than self-realization and improvement. Buddha taught Bandar to become a better person by realizing he was a human being, and that as one he would make mistakes.

Buddha taught him there is no shame in making mistakes as long as you learn from them and move on. Inside these walls he called life, he would be an outcast if he decided to openly practice Buddhism instead of Islam. He would have been immediately run out of the bazaar in an embarrassing way. He and his family would not be safe if his conversion to Buddhism became common knowledge in Bandar Abbas. For your information, my dear reader, this was all before the revolution. Before the revolution, religions other than Islam were freely practiced in Iran; however, it was an unwritten crime to turn from Islam to any other religion, especially one not recognized by Islam. Judaism and Christianity are both mentioned in the Koran, but not Buddhism. This stems from the Islamic belief that it is the last divine religion summoned by God and that every single person on earth should accept it wholeheartedly.

Upon Mr. Bandar's return from Thailand, he brought a few statues of Buddha. He put a couple in his office and kept the rest at his home. In his office he would put the statues out of sight, since they were not so large but very beautiful and meaningful to him. The ones at home were much larger, and he had shipped them from Thailand straight to his front door. (My dear reader, here you decide how many statues Bandar bought and what they were made of and what they looked like.) He would take the statues out of hiding and pay homage to Buddha on a daily basis in his office after lunch. At home he would practice meditation with burning incense in front of his beloved Buddha statues. To find new material on Buddhism, he regularly commuted between Bandar Abbas and Abadan. The latter was an international city, due to the oil business. You could find anything in Abadan freely arriving from all around the world. There was this bookstore owned by an Armenian scholar who carried all sorts of books. The bookstore owner was a short man, and often he would be hidden from sight behind the high stacks of books he had on his shop floor. Everywhere you looked there were books. He had books in many languages, but his main stock of books was in Farsi. He also had many books on Buddhism, which were in Farsi, Japanese, Thai, and Chinese. For specialty books, the Armenian would take orders from Bandar and bring in the books for him. When the books arrived, he would call Bandar, and Bandar would drive to Abadan to buy the books. The Armenian liked Bandar, especially his mannerisms and conduct. The Armenian figured this guy was pretty cool, so what he was reading must be cool too. The Armenian also started reading Buddha's teachings. He was a devout Christian, but soon after reading some of the books, he really liked what Buddha was preaching also.

"Buddha is like Jesus. They both preach the same things, peace and love," the Armenian told Bandar one day, surprising him with his comments.

"Yes, I agree there are similarities, but Buddha never claimed to be the son of God," Bandar replied following a period of silence while he thought about his answer.

"To be honest with you, I don't think Jesus claimed he was son of God. To me he was a good human being who preached goodness and died on the cross for pissing off the wrong people. Others put that label on him for their own benefits." Armenian replied, with a wink and a smile.

Spring and the beginning of summer in 1978 were amazing times for Bandar and his family. The business was flourishing, and Bandar expanded it to Kish Island. He also set up a small shoe store in Kuwait City. He bought the bookstore from the Armenian in Abadan and put his trusted apprentice in charge of the place. His apprentice was this kid who had no family and hung out at the bazaar begging for money and food. The kid was about ten years old when Bandar met him. His parents had died in the sea, and he didn't have any other family in Bandar Abbas. He was originally from Tabriz, which was in Azerbaijan Province northwest of Iran. He and his parents had come for vacation; his parents went to the Persian Gulf for a day of fishing and never returned. There was a massive storm that day, and their boat disintegrated under the heavy lashing of the waves. No boat that size could have survived the carnage. The kid hardly spoke any Farsi, since he spoke only Turkish with his family and in his hometown. Bandar taught him Farsi and took him under his wing and gave him food and money. The kid was brilliant and learned Farsi very quickly. Before long, Bandar gave him a job running deliveries and errands. The kid proved himself not only brilliant, but also trustworthy and hardworking. The kid was soon helping Bandar run his business. After his Thailand trip, Bandar let the kid run the show during his next long vacation, when he took his wife and two sons to Europe during the New Year holiday for three weeks.

In August of that year, Cinema Rex in Abadan was set on fire, and over four hundred people inside were killed. Apparently, it was a well-orchestrated massacre by the radical Islamists. At the time of fire, it was blamed on the shah and his secret service police, SAVAK. After the cinema fire, there was unrest all over Iran. Tehran, the capital city, was buzzing with demonstrations, starting mainly in Tehran University and spreading from there. Then there was the massacre at Jalleh Square in September, where the shah's army opened fire on the demonstrators. The shit hit the fan from that moment on.

"Allah Akbar, Allah Akbar." Allah Akbar (God is Great) was the slogan from the rooftops around Bandar Abbas after dark. Tehran and other larger cities in Iran declared martial law, and Bandar Abbas followed shortly after. *What is the meaning of these slogans and the martial law? Why is everyone shouting Allah Akbar?* Bandar was questioning the events happening around him, and they were happening too fast. His wife put on a scarf and went up the stairs to the rooftop.

"Where are you going?" Bandar asked.

"Going to the rooftop to join everyone else for the fight against oppression. Fight for freedom."

"Why? Why do you want to do that? Are you not happy with your life? Do you know who you want in power instead of shah? What's wrong with what we have? Have you thought what will happen if this government is toppled and the clergy takes over? Do you know who is behind all this?" Bandar machine-gunned these questions, one after another, at his wife. His wife stood there with an "I have no idea what my answer's gonna be" look. She was speechless, and Bandar looked straight back, spearing her eyes with a look of "Well, what do you have to say for yourself?" She took off the scarf and sat down next to Bandar and held his hand, telling him how scared she was and that she didn't want hers to be the only home in the neighborhood not shouting "Allah Akbar." The slogan shouting had been going on now for a few days, and Bandar's family had not gone on the rooftop to participate on any night. The neighbors were asking the wife why they were not joining everyone else on the rooftops. One lady sees Mrs. Bandar in the local market and asks her why there is no Allah Akbar cry coming from their home and how come they have not been seen on their rooftop. She came up with an excuse that her husband was not feeling well, so she has been nursing him, but the neighbor didn't buy it; she has seen Mr. Bandar going to work every day.

"Don't be scared. They cannot harm us for not following," Bandar said, but in fact he was also scared. He was afraid that if he didn't join the uprising, he could lose everything he had worked hard for most of his life in a matter of days. And everything meant *everything*, even their lives as the highest price! That is when he realized Iran was no longer for him and his family, that he needed to take all of them out before it was too late. Tears gathered in his eyes. All he had worked for, all that he owned, all his life here—he had to turn his back on and leave to start somewhere fresh. In a foreign land! The only foreign lands he had seen besides Thailand were Dubai, Istanbul, and London. He loved traveling, but every time out of his home, he longed to come back to it after just a few days. Nowhere else possessed the sounds and smells of his hometown. The gathered tears rolled down his cheeks. His wife's head rested on his chest. His tears rolled down his cheeks onto hers. She looked up and saw the tears rolling from Bandar's eyes. One tear after another, round and moist, in complete silence! She could read in his face that he was planning something. Something that was going to hurt him very much but at the same time would save them. She didn't say anything to him. Just let him be. She grips his hand more tightly and runs her thumb on top of his hand, gently playing with his fingers. He suddenly pressed her hand hard and started to cry, and then to cry and cry some more. *My home, my homeland, my life I am about to lose. It will never be the same again. Not in my lifetime.* The more he thinks about this, the louder he cries. *Will I ever stop crying?*

Khomeini came and executed whoever did not agree with his revolution and Islamic state. He fooled the Iranian people by promising them freedom, but once in power he enforced an Islamic state with a vengeance. Bandar knew this would happen from day one. You cannot trust clergy. Once they get something, it is very hard to get it back from them, and that is exactly what happened. They got the power through Khomeini and to date have not let go.

On the day of voting yes or no for the Islamic state, Bandar voted no, and he was blacklisted right there and then. He knew he could no longer hold on and must leave.

He arranged with his friends to move to Dubai and continue with his business there. He and his family—his wife and three sons—were ready to leave at his command. The kid decided he didn't want to leave Abadan and stayed there running the bookstore. Unfortunately, during the Iran/Iraq war, the bookstore was destroyed in a bombing rampage, and Bandar was saddened but never found out what happened to the kid.

Dubai at the time of Bandar's immigration was underdeveloped, and not much was happening there. Bandar and his family stayed in Dubai and ran their business successfully until the Iran/Iraq war broke out. During the war, the treatment of Iranians in Arabic countries was rude and abusive. Bandar found himself in the middle of this mess in Dubai, and that's when he decided to get the ball rolling toward getting the hell out of the region altogether. News from Iran was downright sad, and he was getting more depressed every day. His hometown of Bandar Abbas was in the midst of the war action, and the port was pretty much shut down. The neighboring cities of Abadan, Ahvaz, and Khoramshahr were destroyed by the meaningless war, and he didn't want to hear anymore. Bandar got himself a good lawyer, and within a year his papers to immigrate to Canada were ready.

He gathered his family after receiving the good news from his lawyer.

"We are going to Canada and the sooner the better. I'm going to get hold of one of my friends who lives in Vancouver and tell him we're coming there. We can stay with him and his family for a while until we get settled." Bandar addressed his family very calmly.

"Who is your friend?" his wife asked.

"His name is Ahmadi. He was a journalist in Tehran, and I visited him many times at his office when visiting Tehran. I loved his magazine, you remember? The one that was in both Farsi and German, with many photos."

His wife is calm and expressionless. "All right, Bandar. Yes, I do know who he is. You know best, my dear. I am sure it will be good. I have faith in you, my dear. You have saved us until now, and I'm sure you will be our savior wherever we go." She adds this with a smile.

Bandar thinks to himself how lucky he is to have this wonderful woman as his wife. She is so understanding and supportive. He cannot imagine a life without her.

Bandar and his family leave Dubai on a beautiful sunny day in fall and arrive on a miserably cold rainy day in Vancouver, after twenty hours of flying and change at Heathrow Airport. Ahmadi was there with a van to pick them up and he takes them to his apartment in West Vancouver, a large three-bedroom condo in a prestigious neighborhood overlooking the water. The rain seemed to be more intense when they got to Ahmadi's place. Bandar and his family were not used to this much rain. They had never experienced rain at this level anywhere they had ever lived. It rained for four days straight. This was the most rain they had ever seen in all their lives!

With the money he had managed to get out of Iran and the money he made in Dubai, Bandar bought a house in a faraway suburb with lots of land. He didn't have any desire to live in the neighborhoods where most Iranians were settling. He preferred to cut all his ties with Iran and, if at all possible, wipe his memory altogether. It hurt him whenever he thought of Iran or heard news about Iran. It saddened him and consequently fouled his mood to a point he was not able to leave his home.

After six months of studying the ins and outs of his neighborhood, he started a small dry cleaning and alteration business in a brand-new strip mall. Once the business was running in full swing, he could not afford to stay home all that often and feel depressed. Since he was on top of his game, his dry cleaning outlet flourished. He expanded by opening two more in other parts of his suburban city. He loved his clientele. They were super friendly, and they always paid. No hassle whatsoever. So different from doing business in Iran. The sons went to school, and his wife helped him with the business and running the alterations side of the enterprise. She was so good with her work that demand for her alteration and tailoring handiwork skyrocketed, and she had to hire two girls on a part-time basis to help her out. Bandar's wife loved her new life of work and helping her husband side by side. She didn't have that opportunity back in Iran. Her only job in Iran was to be a homemaker. It was still a hard and challenging job, but she knew she was better than that. She felt empowered in her new home and environment. She tried very hard to not talk much about Iran, since she knew her husband did not welcome the subject. She talked to him about her customers and the Canadian lifestyle, which was 180 degrees from what they had experienced in Iran. Bandar had not seen this side of his wife in Iran. He realized she was extremely intelligent and very business savvy. She also was not afraid to share her point of view in running the business and expansion plans.

Bandar joined a Buddhist temple and attended the Buddhist rituals and celebrations sponsored by the temple whenever he had the chance. For the longest time, he was the only Persian member of the temple, until another gentleman, much younger than he, joined. He, who was from the beautiful city of Shiraz in Iran. The city of poets, gardens, Persepolis, and wine. Bandar and his newfound friend got along well, and the new guy reminded him of the kid, his apprentice back in Iran.

Bandar had come a long way to be where he is today. He was originally afraid of moving from his homeland to a foreign land where he knew only one person. His fear was proven wrong. He was in a more contented state of mind in his new home than in his past home. Bandar and his family had all become content with their new lives in Canada. They did not have the same lavish lifestyle as in Iran, but they were free, and that was all that mattered to them: freedom.

Ahmadi was also different from the so-called norm in Iran. That's why he and Bandar got along so well despite their very different backgrounds.

Ahmadi was from a prominent family well known for its artists and scholars dating back to the eighteenth century. Their family roots were observed in books, theater, paintings, cinema, poetry, and music. The majority of them taught art and literature in schools and universities across Iran, and some abroad. Ahmadi was a renegade in his own immediate family. He fell in love with journalism and pursued this profession by studying abroad and getting a master's degree in it. He got accepted to the School of Journalism in Tehran and then transferred to Germany for his master's degree. Even though he did not follow in the traditional family fame and fortune, the family respected his decision and supported him all the way. The only thing they could not understand was why Germany?

Ahmadi had always been fascinated with Germans and their culture and language. He specifically loved the German language and how it sounded and rolled on the tongue.

His love for Germany came when he saw a Mercedes-Benz for the first time in the streets of Tehran, followed by a BMW. Ahmadi's dad eventually bought a brand-new Mercedes-Benz, and when Ahmadi was of age, he borrowed it and drove it around Pahlavi Street, showing off and picking up girls with his friends. They would chat up girls walking up and down the street or girls driving around in other cars. They would make a date right there and then head up north of Tehran to Abali for drinks and "Gigar" by the ski slopes.

Ahmadi's main passion was to go to Germany and visit Koln, Munchen, Hamburg, Dusseldorf, Berlin, and Frankfurt. His dad went to Germany many times a year for business. His dad was a talented painter who toured Europe with his artwork and sold them in different galleries in Germany, England, Italy, and Holland. His last stop was always Germany, and if the business was good, he would then drive back to Iran in a brand-new Mercedes-Benz. Whenever Ahmadi's dad returned from Europe, he would bring Ahmadi a gift from Germany. A book, a football magazine, *Spiegel* magazine, and sometimes chocolates! Once and only once, he actually brought a toy: a miniature Mercedes-Benz 300 SL Cabrio! Ahmadi loved his toy car and played with it every day, pretending he was the driver, who was driving a pretty lady around Tehran. The kind of lady one sees in the movies, looking all chic and hip, dragging on a long cigarette: an Audrey Hepburn style of a lady.

Ahmadi's journalism interest was triggered by looking at *Spiegel* at the age of nine. To him *Spiegel* was the ultimate masterpiece in journalism. The way the magazine was laid out with such graphic and vivid pictures. It was real to him. Spiegel did not want to make it pretty. It was a magazine based on hardcore journalism and facts. How did they get those pictures? He would look at the pictures and then try to read the captions in German. Trying to say those long German words was so difficult, but he tried and tried and tried some more every day. Those are such long words. Ahmadi learned English through school. but he wasn't very keen on learning it more, since he just wanted to be fluent in German. *Practice makes perfect*, he kept telling himself. After school every day, he would walk around the front yard and loudly practice German words for hours, until his mother would call him in for supper. After supper he would stay up and finish his homework. His mother thought, *Ahmadi has gone a bit crazy*. She would watch him from the kitchen window and say prayers for him under her breath. By age thirteen Ahmadi had taught himself German, and he was pretty much fluent in reading and writing the language.

He had this friend who was half German on his mother's side and fluent in both German and Farsi. The friend was this cute ten-year-old girl who thought of a world of Ahmadi. Ahmadi was her first crush, this handsome thirteen-year-old true-blood Persian! He would go over to her place and ask her to read the *Spiegel* for him, and she would read the whole magazine to him from front cover to back. She would try to translate whenever she saw his puzzled face, but Ahmadi insisted that she just read on and not stop to translate. She read so well, and even at the tender age of nine her pronunciation was immaculate. He would then very carefully listen to the words and her pronunciation, and he would repeat them over and over again in his head while still listening. G*od, this is so difficult to pronounce! No, it is not! Try it again. Practice, practice, and more practice*!

He wrote his first published piece at the age of sixteen. He wrote it both in Farsi and German. Family and friends were very proud and astounded to see how Ahmadi had excelled in learning German all by himself and how much he enjoyed the language. The whole learning process was a joy for both him and his family. His mother no longer thought he was going crazy, but she still prayed for him under her breath.

After high school Ahmadi went straight to the journalism academy in Tehran. Modern and precise journalism was a new thing to Iran—journalism at the level of *Spiegel*, that is. The academy was a great place to learn the fundamentals. It encouraged students to let their minds run free and get creative in their work. Telling the truth about the politics in Iran during the shah's regime was not encouraged, since it could get a reporter in hot water. There were many underground journalists who contributed to banned underground publications inside and outside of Iran. Ahmadi wanted to be legal but still be able to freely tell the truth. Could that be done there? At that time, no.

The day he opened the letter from Deutsche Journalistenschule reading his acceptance letter to this prestigious journalism school in Germany, he broke down and cried for the first time in his life. He had no reason to cry before then.

Tears were just rolling out of his eyes without any effort. He had absolutely no control over the tears. His hands were trembling, and his whole body felt numb. *I can't believe this. I am crying! I can't believe this! I am going to Munchen. Yay*!

He arrived at the Frankfurt airport on a beautiful sunny morning in September. Aboard the plane he was glued to the window, watching everything outside, even the dark night sky with the flickering wing light. This was not his first time on a plane, but this was a special flight. He was going to Germany. His father was sitting beside him and not bothering Ahmadi, just leaving him be. He was so proud of his son, but he was very traditional and would not show his emotions and say outright to Ahmadi that he was proud. Traditional Persian fathers believed that over praising their children would make them lazy. Praise them for their achievement and reward them just enough as a recognition. Hold back enough from them, so they know there is always room to improve. The Iran Air flight was pleasant. The service on the plane was immaculate. Handsome and pretty air stewardesses were serving drinks and food to all the guests aboard the Boeing 747 Jumbo Jet. What a marvel of engineering this plane is. A massive mass of metal full of people and cargo gets up so smoothly and carries on for miles and lands as smooth as a loon landing on top of a lake. Smooth as silk! The pilot and copilot were both Iranians who were trained by Boeing.

Their connecting flight to Munich was about six hours from the time they arrived in Frankfurt. Ahmadi's dad took him to town; he knew

Frankfurt like the back of his hand. They got on the S-Bun and went to downtown Frankfurt. They got out of the train in Sachsenhausen by the Main River. Ahmadi did not know where to look first. Everywhere he turned there was something incredible to look at. The sights and sounds of this place lifted him up, and he could see himself hovering upward until he had a bird's eye view of the place. *Oh my God, it's so beautiful!* Ahmadi had his arms wide open and was going in a circle, round and round and round nonstop like a Sufi dancer. He was looking down on the rooftops of Sachsenhausen, the top of the boats in the river, and the top of people's heads sitting at the outdoor cafés and bars along the river. This is how it was written in the storybooks. A magical feeling!

"Come on, son, we don't have much time," his father called out. He didn't want to spoil his son's moment, but they were in a rush. He saw his son turning and turning and turning, with his arms stretched wide open on each side of him. He had never seen his son this happy.

Where does he want to go? This is good enough for me, Dad. Please just leave me here for a while, please. His dad started walking away from Ahmadi on the cobblestone sidewalk, and Ahmadi, not by choice, followed. Where was he going? Ahmadi's dad turned into another little street and started walking toward this building that looked like it was built two hundred years ago. An auburn-colored brick building with terraces and flowerpots hanging from each terrace. There was a big sign outside on top of the door with a couple of other signs on the sidewalk, and a beer mug on each sign. *Woohoo, German beer!* Ahmadi was excited and nervous at the same time. *What the hell is my dad up to?*

Ahmadi walked into a bar with his dad in Frankfurt at eleven in the morning. There were many people in this tavern, a very traditional German bar. Suddenly the bartender saw Ahmadi's dad and came over to him and greeted him warmly and shook his hand like they were long-lost friends. He immediately got this gorgeous blonde girl to prepare a table for both Ahmadi and his father. Ahmadi came away from the door and walked inside the tavern to where his dad was getting ready to sit. The waitress was watching him. Ahmadi was wearing a navy blue suit, with a white shirt open at the collar and dark boots. He was an average-looking fellow with great hair, curly and jet black! He also had nice features and bright hazel eyes, but mostly it was his confidence that made him desirable to the opposite sex. Women practically threw themselves at him, but he never took advantage of this and was a gentleman at all times. While walking toward the table, he was looking straight at the girl with the golden hair, emerald eyes, and a ray of sunshine as a smile.

"Bitte." She pulls a chair and points to the chair. He sits down and says, "Danke." *Wow, I spoke German to a German girl in Germany. Yes!*

"Do you know that guy, Dad?" Ahmadi asks his father as he settles in his comfy seat.

"Yes. That is Klaus. He is the co-owner of this place. He owns it with Otto. I also know Otto and Otto's wife, Gertrude. Klaus is not married, but he has many girlfriends," Dad says and immediately bursts into laughter.

Ahmadi's smile conceals a tumult of thoughts. *Wow, my dad is so cool. He knows all these cool people, and we had no idea. I bet dad has partied with Klaus and his "girlfriends" on many occasions. Did Dad cheat on mom? I don't think he would have.* He loved Mom too much. He would have never done such a thing, but, here in Germany with a total stranger, one can never know. It sure doesn't help either that these girls are so damn beautiful. What are these stupid thoughts? Stop it. Who cares if he has or not! It's his business and not anybody else's.

"How do you know all these people dad?" Ahmadi asks.

"Son, you ask too many questions. Let's have a drink. You must be thirsty. I'm sure with all your research and findings about Germany, you must know that they have the best beer in the world, and this tavern has the best beer in Frankfurt."

Beer? What, beer? He wants to have a beer with me? I have never ever had a beer anywhere near my dad, let alone with him.

"Do you want me to have a beer with you, here, right now?" Ahmadi cautiously asks his father.

"Don't you want a beer? We can get anything else you want. You don't have to drink beer if you don't want to. Sorry, son, I just thought you may have had beer in the past and you may like beer," Father replies to Ahmadi with a smile on his face. He knows Ahmadi has had beer and whisky before in Iran, but he has never brought it up with him. Ahmadi never caused any issues inside or outside the house, and when he came home after a night of partying with his friends, he was so cautious to not act drunk it was comical and amusing. His bedroom would wreak with the smell of alcohol the following day, but no one said anything, and Ahmadi thought they just didn't know.

"Well, Dad, I'm not going to lie to you. I would love to have a beer, and yes, I have had beers before when I hung out with friends but nothing heavy, and we never got out of control. Usually, when we went up to Abali to ski, a couple of cold ones were necessary before hitting the slopes."

"I know, my son. We could smell alcohol the following day in your room but not all the time. Your mom would be all upset, and she would ask me to talk to you. I would then only ask her couple of questions to calm her down: "Has he done anything wrong? Did he cause a ruckus?" and she would answer no. So then I would tell her there is no need to talk to him since we both don't see a problem. I assured her if things get out of hand, I would know, and then I would have a chat with you." He laughed.

"Wow, Dad, you guys knew. *Scheiße*! Thanks, Dad, for having my back. Okay, then I will drink anything you are going to have. You know this place and what's good and what's not," Ahmadi told his dad, easing back into his chair. *These are such comfortable chairs*, Ahmadi thought to himself and got really comfortable in his.

His dad pointed to the name of the beer and asked Ahmadi to order two of those. He wanted to hear his son ordering beers in a German tavern in German with perfect pronunciation. He got his wish. Ahmadi motioned to the beautiful frau to come over to their table and take their orders. He then ordered two beers from the beer menu, which were ten pages long. The blonde beauty took the order with a wonderful smile, thanked them, and left. Ahmadi's dad was looking straight at him with pride. His father's gaze sent a good feeling down Ahmadi's spine and gave him goose bumps. He felt the deep love that his dad had for him, right there and then for the very first time without having a single word exchanged between them. He knew his dad loved him, but he hadn't felt it like this until that very moment. He felt so proud of himself and of his dad: *I have such a great man as a father.*

"Thank you, Dad, for letting me order."

"You are welcome. A proud moment for me, my son. I wish your mother was here with us to see this moment. She always had a very special place in her heart for you, my son. I miss her very much," Ahmadi's father says this with a sad sigh. The beers arrive, and once the waitress puts them down on the table, both Ahmadi and his father clink their raised glasses and shout, "Be salamati madar!" (Cheers to Mom).

Ahmadi's mother passed away shortly after she heard the news that her only son was going to Germany for three years. She couldn't stand the thought of being away from her children. She loved her children with all her passion and power. Life had suddenly lost its purpose for her. As soon as she heard the news, she went into her bedroom and cried for days on end.

The shock was too much for her, and she fell ill. Once the pains started, she was diagnosed with cancer, which spread very quickly, and she died within four months. Ahmadi, his sisters, and his father were devastated by her loss, but Ahmadi's dad pulled them together and made sure it was business as usual for the family. Ahmadi felt responsible for his mother's death, and his father didn't want this thought haunting his son for the rest of his life. It was not his fault, and he shouldn't be blamed by anyone, especially himself. The funeral happened too fast, and immediately arrangements were made for Ahmadi to go to Germany. A week after the funeral, both father and son leave Iran for Germany.

"Dad, I miss Mom very much. I think about her every day. She worried about us all the time. I wish she hadn't worried so much. This worrying finally killed her, and there was nothing we could do to stop it," Ahmadi blurted out after taking a long sip of his fine cold beer from this fancy glass. "I wish she was here with us all, free from worry and care. I love you, Dad, and I know you miss her very much. I hope time heals your wounds and you again find yourself a woman to love," Ahmadi says and then thinks to himself *what the fuck did you just say to your dad?*

"I thank you, son! I am not sure if I can find a woman like your mother, so pure, so innocent, and so feminine. I fell in love with her right away, and it was a very strong feeling. I don't think I can love like that again. She was my first and only love, and I will never forget her." His father said this to his son not looking him in the eyes but into the infinite, searching to see his wife's face in the beyond. Ahmadi saw teardrops on his father's cheeks, and he immediately looked away, pretending to not see this. *Wow, this is just too heavy right now.*

"Be salamatiye maman!" Ahmadi lifted his glass again to his mother's memory, and his father did the same thing. "Be salamati azizam!" his father toasted his wife. Ahmadi's dad's eyes were full of tears now, and his chin trembled. He turned his head away from Ahmadi and wiped his eyes with the small handkerchief he always carried in his coat pocket.

"It is okay to cry, Dad. I feel your pain." Ahmadi moved forward and touched his father's knee not taking his eyes off him. His father turned and looked Ahmadi straight in the eyes. He lifted his glass, downed the rest of the beer in one gulp, and called for the girl to bring them two more right away.

They boarded the plane to Munich at the last minute, completely drunk. Both father and son were very similar happy drunks! Laughing and holding each other like two old pals who have just seen each other after a long time. This was the first time he had had so much fun with his dad, and it was not going to be the last one. His father left Ahmadi in Munich and returned to Tehran the following day. He visited Ahmadi twice while he was in Munich, and each time they had an amazing reunion. On his second trip, the father told his son he had met someone he liked and that they were very compatible to. She was a high school teacher in Tehran, and very beautiful. His dad was fifty by then, and his new lady friend was thirty years old.

"Way to go, Dad," Ahmadi said to his father.

"Where did you guys meet?"

"She brought her class to my gallery to see my work. She teaches art to the higher grades. She told me she likes my work and wanted her students to see it up close and at the same time meet the artist. The school called me and asked me if that was okay, and I gave them a time slot when I would be around. When she came in and I saw her, my heart stopped, liked when I met your mom for the very first time." He blushed.

"That day we talked and talked, and she asked me if she could come and talk to me some more and see me at work. I told her she is welcome anytime. We have seen each other every day since. It is such a great feeling to feel love again my son."

"Ah, Dad, I am so happy for you. I was hoping this would happen to you. You are a wonderful man, with so much love and passion, and you were being wasted. You have made me the happiest son ever, Dad." Ahmadi jumped over and gave him a big hug. He got squeezed back just as hard and passionately.

"Do you have a picture of her?" Ahmadi asked.

His dad took out a picture of them in northern Iran at a famous Caspian Sea resort, Motel Ghoo (the Swan Motel), and handed it over to his son.

"Wow, Dad, she's beautiful. She has such a kind face! God, I am so happy for you, Dad. This is so amazing."

"Next time I come, I will bring her with me," Ahmadi's dad told him. He took the picture back and put it back in his wallet, right next to the picture of Ahmadi's mother that he has been carrying now forever. Ahmadi thought it is so ironic that his mom and this lady looked so much alike. *I wish you all happiness my dear dad.*

"I will be back before you know it, Dad. Have you forgotten this is my last term here? I am going to get my master's in exactly three more months, and then I will be back home," he told his father gleefully. As much as Ahmadi loved Germany, he was longing for the sites and sounds of Iran and his friends. He missed home!

Journalism school in Munich was everything that he had imagined it to be. Hard, strict, precise, demanding, fun, and lots and lots of work—true German! He loved being pushed around and challenged by the professors and some of the senior German students who were brilliant. It was also a school of hard knocks—a kick-your-ass, in-your-face attitude. However, when you did great work, you were deservedly recognized and praised. This trait of the Germans was so commendable. One day one of his professors showcased his work and told the class that they could use it as an example to complete their work. He beat all the Germans and got the highest mark in that class. That was a proud moment for Ahmadi. In that moment he knew there were no obstacles in life that he could not overcome. Life was beautiful.

Graduation was lots of fun. It was a drunkfest from morning of the day of graduation to the morning after the graduation ceremony. Ahmadi woke up the next afternoon in his girlfriend's house in the outskirts of Munich. He would never forget that day, even with the extreme hangover that he was nursing. Most memories were blurred, but they were still there, especially memories of this beauty he was going to leave behind. *No time to think right now. Let's gather my stuff and get the hell out of here. I have a train to catch.*

Ahmadi went exploring Europe before returning to Iran. He visited Frankfurt and Köln in Germany and then made his way to Venice, Amsterdam, Paris, and London! Upon his return to Iran, he worked very hard to make money, in order to go back to Europe. His second trip was in 1978, when he visited Barcelona, Lisbon, and Athens with the money he made working as an up-and-coming young journalist in Iran. Two years before his second trip, he had been arrested by SAVAK, the shah's secret service police, and put in jail for a year for an article he wrote criticizing the Pahlavi policies. He was freed because of the status of his family and their ties in Iran. His prolonged imprisonment could also raise a stink for the ruling family. Still, he was jailed for a year for practicing freedom of speech.

Ahmadi's welcome-home party at Mehrabad airport when he returned to Iran after completing his master's was excessive. Every aunt, uncle, and cousin was there to welcome him back home. They were all so proud of their boy. The first in the family to get a masters degree! A journalism master's degree from a prestigious school in Germany! That was a huge deal for the family. Ahmadi could not believe the chaos in Mehrabad airport. People were climbing over one another to greet their loved ones coming out in a single file through the sliding doors after clearing customs. Ahmadi could hear his name being called by hundreds of different voices coming from every direction. His head was going from right to left, up to down. *Wow, what a difference between here and Germany!* In Germany this type of chaos was nonexistent. He had been in many airports in Germany, and he never saw anything like this in any of them. *Why are we like this?* Ahmadi asked himself while pushing his baggage trolley through a sea of people. He felt suffocated by the crowd pushing him from all sides while he tried to get out of this single file of people moving forward at a snail's pace. The single file was barricaded by metal stands to keep the welcoming parties out of the path of travelers coming out. The single file got tighter and tighter by the pushing of people on the barricades from each side. People had no regard for one another, so it seemed.

He finally got out of the mayhem and saw his father and the rest of the family piling up on top of one another in order to be the first ones to say hello. He greeted each one and kissed them all on their cheeks. He held the children and kissed them and gave hugs to the older kids. He didn't even know some of these people. He had been away for awhile.

There were people coming and going for about a week to greet him and welcome him back home—Ahmadi's family and friends, friends of friends, and also friends of his dad and his new stepmother. His dad was now married to his second wife, the schoolteacher. Such a wonderful lady. Ahmadi took a liking to her right away. Her resemblance to his mother was mind-blowing. She even talked and walked like her. It was like his mom's spirit had crossed over into this lady.

Ahmadi wined and dined and rested up for one week, and after that week it was time to work and be serious. He didn't want to work for any of the local papers, since they were all censored; censorship did not sit so well with Ahmadi. With the financial help of his father and his uncle, he started his own magazine in Iran, a German/Persian monthly magazine that featured German and Persian culture, music, fashion, literature, and tourism. It also had a front page editorial written by Ahmadi that tackled Iran's politics. It was the only mention of any politics, domestic or foreign, in the entire magazine.

The magazine took off from its first edition. It was called *Aknun/Nun*, which means "Now," both in Farsi and in German! *Aknun/Nun* was printed in both Farsi and German; the front half was in Farsi, and the back half was in German. The same stories and subjects were covered in both languages. Ahmadi hired talented writers who were fluent in Farsi and German. He also acquired the help of a few German expatriates who were working and living in Iran who were interested in contributing to his magazine as writers or editors. He modeled his magazine after *Spiegel*, colorful and full of substance, with lots and lots of pictures! In one of his issues, Ahmadi ran an editorial regarding the trial of Golesorkhi in Tehran defending some of Golesorkhi's ideology of freedom from a totalitarian regime and oppression. Ahmadi believed that everyone was entitled to their opinions and should not be prosecuted for their political beliefs. Golesorkhi's trial and execution made him very angry, and the editorial that he wrote got him in hot water with SAVAK. His editorial called on the shah to remove the government's restrictions on political freedom. Mohammad Reza Pahlavi had outlawed communism, under pressure from the United States. The USA and its Western allies were very afraid of the Soviet Union's influence on Iran. They did everything they could to keep communism out of Iran. Iran becoming communist meant bye-bye to the Western influences in the region. Iran becoming a communist state meant the Soviet Union becoming more influential in the oil-rich region, and that was extremely dangerous to the capitalist ideology and its adherents.

The majority of political prisoners in Iran during the shah's reign were communists with ties to the Soviet Union. The biggest mistake the shah ever made in his political career was to listen to outsiders, unlike his father Reza Pahlavi, who told outsiders to fuck off, which was also the ground for his downfall and exile.

Ahmadi's article called on the government to free political prisoners and slowly introduce free elections for members of the government and cabinet. SAVAK was at his doorstep two days after the editorial was published. *Aknun/Nun* was shut down, and Ahmadi was arrested, along with many of his reporters and support staff. He begged SAVAK to let his staff go. He argued that whatever was published in his magazine was under his direct supervision, and they just followed his orders. But SAVAK would not listen to his cries and destroyed his office and took everyone, except the Germans, to prison. Ahmadi was tried and found guilty of publishing banned material, poisoning the minds of his countrymen.

He was sentenced to five years in prison under harsh conditions at the infamous Evin prison. He was freed after serving just over one year, because of his family's influence on the royal family. During that year in hell, he was tortured and beaten on various occasions by prison guards who had nothing else to do. Many and so Many Iranians demonstrated against his imprisonment in the streets of Tehran, Isfahan, Shiraz, and Tabriz. He was released under the condition that he could never own a publication in Iran and that if he wanted to pursue his journalism career, he could do so only through the established newspapers and magazines, which bowed down to the government censorship. He was arrested in the spring of 1975 and released in the summer of 1976.

When he was released from jail, he was frail and thin. There were dark circles around his eyes, and his cheeks pulled in, since he had lost many teeth in prison. His aunt broke down in tears when she saw him. She and couple of his friends had come to pick him up. Ahmadi's father was banned from going to prison by the family, since he could not hold his tongue and would have gotten both himself and Ahmadi in more trouble. He cursed the system and the prison guards every day, from sunrise to sundown. When they arrived at Ahmadi's apartment, his father was there waiting for him, and he stayed with Ahmadi for few weeks, taking care of his weakened son. It took Ahmadi a whole year to fully recover from the horrific experience of imprisonment. When Ahmadi got his strength back, he decided he needed to get out of Iran again for awhile. That's when he went back to Europe.

He returned to Iran when talk of revolution was in the air. The shah was in his last days of power, and the rumor was that the shah was leaving Iran, while the great leader Ayatollah Khomeini was on his way back after many years in exile. Ahmadi was excited about this new buzz in Iran. He, like many others, was hoping for a change from the present suppression to a more relaxed Iran, which will would lead to a completely free Iran.

The shah left the country and appointed one of his arch enemies, Mr. Bakhtiar, as his prime minister while he was away. The very first thing Bakhtiar did was to free political prisoners and grant freedom of the press. Ahmadi jumped on the freedom bandwagon and reopened his publication with the help of his father. Ahmadi's father did not share his son's optimism regarding the upcoming changes; as a matter of fact, he was quite worried. Ahmadi's father liked the present situation with Bakhtiar as prime minister, but he knew it was going to be shortlived, once Khomeini got back into

Iran. Ahmadi assured him that the winds of change were on the wings of Iran's symbolic bird, Homa, and these changes were going to make their country the best in the world. As a matter of fact, his first-issue cover photo of the reopened publication showed Homa spreading its wings over a map of Iran, with the word "Change" in Farsi and German written on each wing.

Khomeini arrived in Tehran, and thousands upon thousands of people lined the airport and the streets of Tehran to welcome their revolutionary leader. Ahmadi decided to stay home with his father and watch the historic return on television. Ahmadi never forgot his father's blank look when he heard Khomeini answer a reporter's question on the Air France flight back to Tehran just before touching down. The reporter asked Khomeini what he was feeling now that was returning to Iran after so many years of exile. Khomeini's answer was "Hitchi" (nothing)! *Nothing?* Ahmadi said it under his breath and then immediately looked toward his dad. His dad was staring at the television set with his mouth wide open, with the scariest look Ahmadi had ever seen. It looked like Ahmadi's father had suffered a stroke right there and then, frozen after hearing Khomeini's "Hitchi." After a couple of minutes of silence and that look, Ahmadi's father got up in a rage and screamed out the word *hitchi* over and over again. "What the fuck do you mean, *hitchi*, you son of a bitch? You are coming back to your own country after so many years in exile, and people are going to look up to you and follow you, and you say you have no feelings? You piece of shit, you! Ahmadi's dad is furious and walks out of the house still shouting and cursing the ayatollah. There and then Ahmadi knew his dad was right about Khomeini and his intentions."

Ahmadi published two more editions of his magazine before it was shut down again, this time by Khomeini's revolutionary guards. Bakhtiar had run away to France, and Khomeini had formed an Islamic state. Islamic state? That's not freedom. How can we have freedom within an Islamic state? Fortunately, this time, unlike the first time he was shut down by SAVAK, Ahmadi was not arrested. The authorities told him the publication was temporarily shut down, until its contents were reviewed by the revolutionary council. According to them, the contents must meet the requirements of the Islamic revolution, Islamic state, and new constitution. Ahmadi knew his magazine would not have a hope in hell of passing the requirements as they were stated. He closed down his journalism office and started teaching German as a private tutor until he got a job with a prestigious university abroad.

Ahmadi packed his bags again, and this time he left for Canada and not Germany. He got himself a prestigious associate professor job at the UBC school of Journalism.

Ahmadi adjusted to Canada very quickly. He found Vancouverites to be such laid-back and understanding people. Very little ignorance and arrogance! The first thing that impressed him was that he learned that all the professors are called by their first names, even if they have a PhD in nuclear physics. A guy is still called Brad, not Doctor, Engineer, or Mr. Bradley Henderson. He loved that about the Canadian culture. Very different from the Iranian way! In Iran anyone with a PhD was considered a god and was referred to always as Doctor. One was never referred to by first name. Even some men's wives called their husbands Doctor, which was totally ridiculous. No wonder the Canadians were more advanced and chill. They didn't differentiate between individuals based on their level of education and status. Everyone was equal as members of the society. People thought communism's ultimate goal was to bring this equality, but that didn't really work out either. In Canada if you have a PhD, deservedly you make more money than someone who is a laborer; but the one with the PhD is referred to by his first name, same as the laborer.

After a few years of hard work, Ahmadi managed to save money and purchase a comfortable apartment in Vancouver near UBC. He owned a large three-bedroom apartment on the top floor of a newer building located on a beautifully tree-lined street. He had an amazing view of the North Shore Mountains from his bedroom. It was the view that initially made him fall in love with the suite. After viewing the place, he immediately put an offer on it. Ahmadi was also car-free. He traveled by bus or, when the weather was favorable, with his bicycle to and from the university. Most of his friends had cars, so he would hitch a ride here and there with them when meeting up with his friends for a night out in town or if he had to travel far.

He met the love of his life on the bus to UBC. She was a student at the university, and he saw her nearly every time he took the bus. As soon as he laid eyes on her, he knew she was the one. Cupid was flying around and saw Ahmadi getting on the bus that day. Cupid chose him. Every day Cupid falls for a different person, and that day Cupid fell in love with Ahmadi's kind face. Cupid took an arrow and looked around for the right match for

Ahmadi. Cupid found her, aimed at Ahmadi's heart, and shot the arrow, and it went right through. Very seldom does an arrow go right through. Cupid was so proud: this was a perfect match. Ahmadi made the initial eye contact, and she looked back. This went on for a month, Monday to Friday. After a month of glances, smiles were mixed in. She smiled first. He smiled back and got red in the face. He was so embarrassed he turned around. He felt like a schoolboy meeting his first crush. From that day on, he smiled every time he saw her on the bus, and she would return his smile warmly. It was ironic; they were never close enough on the bus to spark a conversation, since the bus was so overcrowded. Ahmadi took the bus closer to the beginning of the line, and she, closer to the end. He would look for her at the university during his breaks, but no sign of her in all the usual spots around the campus. One day he was looking for a book in the library, and suddenly he had a gut feeling she was nearby. Right then he heard her voice.

"Hello. My name is Sahra. I see you on the bus all the time. Are you a student here?"

"Hi. I go by Ahmadi. Sahra, is that a Persian name? It means Sahara in English," Ahmadi replied.

"Yes, I know. I am half Persian. My father is Persian, and my mom is German," she replied with a smile.

"I am Persian too. Nice. I am full Persian, but I went to university in Germany. I have a master's degree in journalism, and I am an associate professor here at the university." Ahmadi extended his hand to shake hers. "Very nice to meet you, Sahra. Do you speak both Farsi and German?"

"I speak fluent German, but my Farsi is not so good. I understand it better than I speak it. My dad speaks either English or German to me, and the only person who spoke Farsi with me was my grandma, who recently passed away."

"God bless her. I lost both my grandmothers awhile back. They were such lovely ladies. I miss them very much," Ahmadi said. "Can we please speak in German? I miss speaking German. It has been awhile since I have spoken it with someone who is fluent."

"Natürlich," she replied. They talked about Germany and their favorite places there and Ahmadi's life in Iran before coming to Vancouver—right there in one of the aisles in the library. The entire conversation was in German. They completely lost track of time, and Ahmadi realized he still needed to find the material at the library. He asked Sahra if she would like to join him for dinner at this new trendy restaurant near campus. She agreed and they parted ways.

A year later Ahmadi married Sahra in a simple ceremony in Vancouver. They held an even smaller ceremony in Germany for Sahra's family and some of Ahmadi's friends. Ahmadi's father, his father's wife and Ahmadi's sisters also attended the ceremony in Germany. Ahmadi's father was so proud of his son for marrying such a beautiful and bright woman. He always knew his son would marry a *fereshte,* an angel. After the ceremony in Germany, they took off to Cuba for their honeymoon. Ahmadi had fond memories of Cuba from his last trip there. He went to Cuba solo one fall and had the best time of his life. He particularly loved Cuban culture, music, and women. He was not much of a cigar smoker, but he had one or two Cuban cigars and even enjoyed those stogies while sipping on a glass of fine Cuban rum.

Their honeymoon was amazing. Sahra loved everything about the Cuban culture and the beautiful sandy beaches. They made love, drank exotic drinks, snorkeled, went sightseeing around the island, and made more love. Their first child was conceived in Cuba. They returned to Vancouver full of love and happiness. Upon their return to Vancouver, Ahmadi continued with his work at the university, and Sahra continued with her studies. She wanted to get her doctorate, and that was still a few years away. Meanwhile, for extra money, she helped out in the university as a TA and provided private tutoring. (My dear reader, you decide what Sahra was studying at the university and what doctorate she wanted to obtain, and let me know.)

A few months after the birth of their first child (dear reader, please determine the gender of their firstborn), one evening when they were holding each other and watching their favorite program on TV, *Monday Night Football,* they heard a knock on the door. They thought perhaps it was someone from the building, since the building was secure, and one could get in only if buzzed in. Who could it be this time of night? Ahmadi got up and walked toward the door while Sahra was waiting for the last play of the half to take place. Ahmadi opened the door.

"Hello, are you Ahmadi?" a beautiful young girl asked.

"Yes. And you are …?"

"My name is Henni. My mother's name is Hedda. You know her. She told me you are my father." She said this very calmly and extended her left hand to shake Ahmadi's. "I have come from Germany to visit with you."

"You are my daughter? Is this a joke? How come I didn't know about this? Are you serious?" Ahmadi's shocked look scared Henni, and she moved back. Ahmadi realized he must have scared the girl with his tone of voice and look. He gently took Henni's hand in his and brought her inside, and they both walked toward the living room.

"Sahra, my dear. We have a guest. This is Henni. She tells me that she is my daughter. She just arrived from Germany," Ahmadi calmly called to Sahra, who was on her feet, glued to the television set, waiting for the last play.

"Who? What? Your daughter? How?" Sahra fired back, not sounding mad but more concerned, and still glued to the TV set.

"I am not sure how to answer that, Sahra. Let Henni do the talking," Ahmadi replied.

Henni came forward and extended her hand toward Sahra. Sahra finally took her eyes off the TV screen and looked to Henni. Sahra grabbed Henni's extended hand and shook it. "Hi, my name is Sahra. I am his wife." She turned back to the TV screen. "Please give me one second. I will explain later." Sahra hushed Henni when Henni started to talk. Henni did not say anything and looked at the TV screen also. The final play was over, and Sahra grunted and looked at Henni. She said, "Okay, you were saying, my dear …"

"Hi, my name is Henni. I am his daughter. Please don't be alarmed. I didn't come here to get anything from him. I just wanted to meet my dad. My mother, Hedda, told me the truth about him a year ago. When I was growing up, she told me my real father was killed in Iran when he went back. My mother has been married now for many years, and I have two half-brothers," she tells both of the stunned onlookers. "A year ago my mother found out that my dad was still alive when she came across an article written by him in a university journal. She then felt obligated to tell me the truth. I decided I wanted to meet my dad, so now I am here."

"How did you get into the building?" Ahmadi finally asked.

"I only could find your building number and not the unit number. At the front door of the building, this nice security guard let me in and asked me who I was looking for. When I told him I was here to see you, he buzzed me up to your floor and walked me to your front door. He left when I knocked. Did I do something wrong?"

Henni was a very pretty young lady. She could not be more than twenty-one or twenty-two. She had Ahmadi's eyes and chin, and the rest was her mother's. She was tall and slender like Ahmadi. She is also a good dresser, just like her father.

"No, you didn't do anything wrong. Please sit down, my dear. You have had a long journey," Sahra said to Henni in German.

"Oh, you speak German? Nice." Henni smiled, and, oh, that smile was definitely Ahmadi. No doubt!

"Yes. Like you, I am half German and half Persian," Sahra replied, again in German. "Please sit down. Can I get you anything?"

"A beer, please, if it is no trouble."

"How old are you, Henni? The drinking age here is nineteen." Ahmadi made sure he was not going to give beer to a minor.

"I am twenty-one, Dad. I will be twenty-two next week. I wanted to spend my birthday with you," she answered, taking her passport out of her purse and handing it to Ahmadi. Ahmadi suddenly got a chill up his spine. He became a father when he was twenty-five years old, and until today he'd had absolutely no idea.

The name on the passport was Henni Rebekah Ahmadi. She has the same last name as me. How did she get away with that? Nobody asked me if this is okay with me.

"Henni, yes, I do know your mother, Hedda. She and I were together for over a year. I went back to Iran, and then from there I came to Canada. I asked her to come with me to Iran, but she refused. After that she never contacted me. I tried hard to find her again, but she completely disappeared from my life—and now this." Ahmadi paused. "I am not sure how I'm feeling right now. I know I feel somehow betrayed by your mother. She should have told me. You show up out of nowhere and knock on my door and tell me you are my daughter. This is a bit hard for me to digest right now." Ahmadi leaned back on his chair and reached for his pipe. Ahmadi had taken up pipe smoking, since he loved the smell of pipe tobacco and seriously wanted to quit smoking cigarettes.

"Where are you staying?" he asked after lighting up his pipe, breaking an awkward silence.

"I have a motel room not far from here." Henni answered, her head down.

Sahra suddenly jumped into the conversation. "You can't be staying in a motel when we have extra rooms here. I will come with you to the motel and we will grab your stuff and bring you here. You are going to stay here with us."

After that comment, Ahmadi stared at Sahra as if to say, "What the hell did you just say?"

"Can I please speak with you a minute alone, Sahra?" Ahmadi got up and walked toward the kitchen. Sahra got up and followed him. In the kitchen, Ahmadi threw a hissy fit with his hands up and shaking his head. Sahra had never seen Ahmadi this troubled.

"Are you out of your mind?" Ahmadi asked in a hushed voice. "Are you serious? Do you really want a total stranger staying in our home? We have no idea who she really is and what she is capable of doing."

"She is your daughter, Ahmadi. Can't you see? She has your eyes, your chin, your laugh, your manners. She *is* you. I don't know how you don't see this. I am going to be responsible for her, okay? If anything goes wrong, blame me. There is something about this girl that bedelam neshast." She reverted to Farsi to express how she had just taken a strong liking to the girl.

"You are weird, my love. Any other woman would have been upset with this scenario, and here, you want her to stay in our home. Weird!" He threw his hands up in the air. "Okay, it's your call. You want her to stay, then, I guess she is staying." He opened the door to the living room from the kitchen. Henni was gone. She had left, and in their heated conversation in the kitchen, they didn't hear her leave. Ahmadi ran toward the front door of the apartment. No sign of Henni. He went down to the lobby and asked security if he saw a girl leave. The security told him she had just left the building. Ahmadi rushed outside and saw Henni walking fast away from the building.

"Henni, wait, please wait. Don't go. Please stay, my child. Please stay," Ahmadi shouted while running after her. Henni stopped but didn't turn around. She just stopped walking with her head down. Ahmadi finally caught up to her and held her in her arms.

"Come, my child. Let's go and get your stuff from the motel. You are going to stay with your family."

"I don't want to cause you and your wife any problems, Father. I can go and never return. I just wanted to meet you, to know that you really exist."

"Now that you have found me, you want to leave so quickly? No, my child. I want to get to know you. You are my daughter." He gave her a big kiss on the forehead. They walked slowly back to the apartment building without saying another word.

"Welkommen," Sahra told Henni as soon as she entered the house. "Let's go and get your stuff from the motel." Sahra said to Henni, "I will take her. You stay and relax, my dear." Sahra tells Ahmadi.

"Before you go, Henni, please give me the number for your mom. I want to talk to her," Ahmadi said.

"Here is her business card, Father." She hands him a business card. It's a number in Essen. *Essen, what the hell is she doing in Essen?*

After Sahra and Henni left, Ahmadi called Hedda.

"Hello, jah" a woman's voice came on the phone.

"Hello, is this Hedda?" Ahmadi asked in German.

"Yes, who is this?" Hedda's sounded irritated.

"Hi, Hedda. It is me, Ahmadi. Our daughter paid me a visit today." He came right to the point.

"Oh my God, a blast from the past. How are you? Henni? She is with you?"

"She is not with me right now. She has gone with my wife to get her belongings from the motel she is staying at. She came here to visit me. Why didn't you tell me about her, Hedda? By the way, she is stunning." Ahmadi was in tears now.

"Oh, my dear Ahmadi. Congratulations on your marriage. She must be a good woman to be with you. Ah Ahmadi, my dear. What can I say? Shortly after you left, I found out I was pregnant. I guess we didn't practice safe sex that night." She laughed. "Anyway, I was pregnant and alone. I didn't know where to find you or even how to find you. I left Munich and came to Essen. Here I have lots of family, and I worked at one of my cousin's farms in the outskirts of Essen. It was good work, and I needed the money. But it was very physical and heavy work. I felt if I continued, I may lose the child, and I didn't want that to happen. That child is my everlasting memory of you. I loved you very much, Ahmadi, but I just couldn't go away with you. I am not a risk taker like you. To this day I still love you.

"At five months pregnant, I quit the farm job and started working with a real estate agent, helping with her administration work. After taking a month off work after giving birth to Henni, I went back to work with the same lady, and every day I took Henni with me to work. I took her everywhere I went. I didn't want to lose sight of her for even one second. She so much reminded me of you, and she was also such a good baby. Always smiling and the only time she cried was when she either wanted food or changing.

"When Henni was two, I took my real estate course and became a real estate agent in Essen. I made a good living, and the bonus about this line of work was that I could take Henni to work with me. It was the only profession I could have her with me without hearing complaints. I am semiretired now. I made enough money to make myself a healthy nest egg. By the way, Henni never told me she was coming to see you. She kept that hidden from me that little rascal." Hedda laughed again.

"She is very beautiful, Hedda. She has taken all our good features." Ahmadi laughs. "What does she do in Germany? Does she live with you or by herself?"

"She lives with me, but she is very independent. She is also a smarty-pants, just like her father. She finished her high school at the age of sixteen and got a scholarship at the Goethe University for architecture. She is an architect, Ahmadi. She is not working right now, since she just got her degree, but many companies are after her. Her school project was number one in the whole of Germany. I am so proud of my girl."

"Our girl! You are very proud of *our* girl." He laughs again. "May I keep her here for a while? May I do that, please?"

"If she wants to stay with you and your family is okay with that, I have no objections. She is a grown woman, and she doesn't need my permission. Plus, she is with her dad. I am very happy she has come to visit you."

"She tells me you got married and have two boys."

"Yes, I did get married, and I have two boys from the marriage. My husband passed away after the birth of my second son. He was sick from the day I met him, but I loved him and stayed with him. He was an amazing man, very much like you, Ahmadi. Henni liked him very much too, but she knew very well he was not her dad. So one day out of the blue, she asked me, and I told her that my husband was not her real dad, that her real dad was an Iranian who went back to Iran. I also said because of his political beliefs, he was caught and executed. I didn't know what else to tell her at that time. I didn't know if you were dead or alive until I saw your article in one of the university journals she brings home with her. That's when I told her more about you, and that's when she decided she wanted your last name on hers. She made all the decisions herself, Ahmadi."

"I believe it. Well, dear, I have to let you go now. They should be coming back any minute now. I will have her call you, and you guys can talk. Have a wonderful day, Hedda. It was great talking to you."

"You too, my dearest. Your wife is a very lucky lady to be with you. How did she take the news about Henni?" Hedda asked.

"She took it much better than I did. She told Henni that she is going to stay with us instead of in a motel, and now she has taken her to the motel to get her stuff. I am married to a wonderful woman, Hedda. She is kind, generous, beautiful, smart, and funny. She makes me laugh every day, and I can't thank her enough. By the way, her name is Sahra, which means desert in Farsi."

"Beautiful name. I'm happy you found a good match, Ahmadi. Please take care, and I hope one day soon I see you again."

They said their goodbyes and hung up.

Ahmadi went to make one of the spare bedrooms ready for his daughter. He chose the best one, the one with a large window opening to the garden in front of the building. Lots and lots of natural light in this room! He wants her stay to be super special. *I hope she stays a long time with me. I am sure I can get her a job through my contacts here.* He made the bed ready and emptied the closet, making room for Henni's belongings.

Meanwhile, a few blocks away, Sahra and Henni are at the motel where Henni got herself a single room. Not a large room but a cozy one with a queen-size bed, a TV, and a lamp. The closet has drawers built in it, since there is not enough room for a stand-alone dresser in the room. There is a window that opens to the gardens behind the motel. Within a short distance from the window are few bird houses, full of different-colored birds feeding. The sight of birds feeding gave Sahra a sense of calm. A serene feeling came over her, and she felt incredibly happy. The happiest she had been in a long time. With the arrival of Henni, she felt excited. Excited and motherly at the same time! She was six months pregnant with their first child, and she was looking forward to having another girl in the house who could speak German and was a blood relative of her only true love. It couldn't get any better than this.

Henni grabbed her suitcase from the inside of the closet and started putting her clothes and other personal items inside it. Sahra went to the washroom and started to grab Henni's toiletries. Everything was from Germany. Sahra was beaming with excitement, picking up different products and reading the labels loudly. Hair products, shampoo, conditioner, toothpaste, deodorant, and makeup. It seemed Henni did not use too much makeup, since she didn't have many items. *Is it because she doesn't like wearing makeup or simply she cannot afford it since makeup in Germany is very expensive?* After helping Henni pack her belongings, Sahra told Henni that she will be out in the lobby waiting for her. Henni went through the entire room making sure that she hasn't left anything behind. She had a habit of always leaving something behind when she was away.

After the thorough check, Henni grabbed the suitcase and headed toward the front desk. She handed the key to the front desk attendant and asked for her bill.

"Your friend paid for your room," the front desk attendant told Henni. Henni thanked the attendant and went out into the parking area where Sahra was waiting by the car. Henni thanked Sahra for paying her bill but insisted that she not do that again. She did not feel comfortable with someone else paying her bills. Sahra apologized to Henni and assured her that she would not do this again. Sahra told Henni it's a Persian thing.

"So you want to tell me Persians pay each other's bills? I should move to Iran then," Henni said jokingly.

"You have a lovely smile, Henni."

"Thank you. People tell me that," Henni replied with another smile.

Henni and Sahra made the best of the short drive back to the house. Sahra told Henni how she met Ahmadi and how it was love at the first sight.

"I met him on the bus. I would see him and smile at him, and he would smile back. He was so shy I actually had to approach him myself and introduce myself to him one day in the library. I thought he was a graduate student, but then I found out he is an associate professor at such a young age."

"You believe in love at first sight?" Henni asks

"I didn't before, but I experienced it firsthand. When I saw your dad for the first time I knew right there and then that I was going to love this man. Don't ask me how, but I just knew." Sahra replied while looking to her right and left while driving. Sahra knew that she was not a good driver. She got nervous behind the wheel. She had a phobia that she was going to cause an accident or be in one. Henni noticed Sahra's nervousness.

"Are you all right, Sahra?" Henni asked with a concerned voice.

"Yes, I am fine. I don't like driving, and I get nervous every time I drive. I have never been in an accident, and I have this fear that one day I will get into one," Sahra replied.

"I have been in two accidents in my life, Sahra. One time my fault and the other time not. The one which was my fault I was speeding on a rural street, and I lost control of my car on a curve and went through a front door of a house. The second one, this guy ran a red light and hit me right in the middle of my car. I believe in North American slang, it is called T-boned. Both time no major injuries to anyone, which is a blessing. These days I get some aches and pains in my shoulders and neck, but nothing too serious," Henni says to Sahra.

"While I was going to university, I was making some money by giving therapeutic massages. I am a certified masseuse. I can help you. On top of that, I know a thing or two about holistic medicine, which can also be helpful," Sahra replied with a smile. Henni smiled back and thanked Sahra for all her kindness. Henni was smiling more since Sahra told her she has a beautiful smile.

They got back when the Monday night football was in the last minutes. Ahmadi was glued to TV and didn't hear the girls coming back home. His favorite team, the Washington Redskins, was playing against their arch rival, the New York Giants. The Giants, unfortunately, were ahead, and there was no chance for Washington to catch up. Ahmadi heard noise coming from the kitchen and left the game to go investigate. He greeted the ladies with a smile and grabbed the bags and showed Henni to her room. Meanwhile, Sahra was preparing a sandwich for Henni in the kitchen.

"It is such a beautiful room, Dad. Thank you." Henni hugged Ahmadi, and Ahmadi hugged her back.

Henni's stay extended over what she had originally anticipated. Both Ahmadi and Sahra didn't want her to leave. Moving around for pregnant Sahra was becoming more difficult, and Henni was doing all the housework and the shopping. They were so grateful for her being there. Sahra, on a beautiful fall day, gave birth to a baby boy, and Henni stayed on even longer, helping Sahra with the newborn. (My dear readers please name Ahmadi's new baby boy.)

After a few months, Bandar and his family finally came over to Ahmadi's home to congratulate him and his lovely wife on their newborn. When they arrived they immediately noticed Henni, and Bandar jokingly told Ahmadi he had hired a very pretty girl for a nanny.

"She is my daughter, Bandar jan. She is my daughter with the woman I used to date in Germany. Her name is Henni. She has been here for few months now, and Sahra and I are very grateful for her being here," Ahmadi explained to Bandar.

Bandar was totally taken off guard by the uncanny explanation of Ahmadi. Ahmadi very calmly just announced in front of me and my family that he has an illegitimate daughter with another woman and that has been and currently is all right with him and his wife. Bandar explained Henni to his family, and immediately Bandar's wife went to the kitchen to talk to Sahra.

"Sahra jan, I just heard from my husband the situation with the blonde girl here. Are you all right?" Bandar's wife asked Sahra.

"Of course I am fine, dear. I can't be any better. Oh, Henni is a blessing. She is so nice. She is just like Ahmadi. I don't know what I would have done without her here. She has helped me so much with the work around the place, with shopping, and now with our little one. I am so grateful," Sahra replied calmly while making a delicious mastokhiar (Szatzki Persian style).

"So you mean to tell me you don't mind knowing your husband had an affair with another woman," Bandar's wife said.

"Ahmadi did not have an affair with anyone. He had girlfriends in the past, which is totally understandable. Accidents do happen, and as a result a beautiful person was created. Henni is a female Ahmadi. Considerate, beautiful, kind, and smart. I am thankful for that accident, and so is he. Ahmadi treats Henni as a daughter, and I treat her as a good friend. It is a win-win situation for all of us. My husband has been true to me since the day we met, so I have nothing to worry about." Sahra still calmly went about her business in the kitchen.

"You are amazing, Sahra. I wish I was as strong as you. I look up to you, my friend. Your friend is also my friend. I will treat Henni also as a friend. Thank you so much for enlightening me again." Bandar's wife gave Sahra a big smile and a hug and went back to the living room.

In the living room, Bandar's eldest son, now thirty years old, was chatting up Henni. A handsome fellow, the tallest in the family at six feet, he was also a charming fellow. Women loved him; his charm was captivating, and he said the nicest and sweetest things. He told women what they liked to hear; in two dates he would have them in his grasp. He knew it too. It was like a game for him. Chase them, charm them, sleep with them, and then either keep them around or axe them. Henni was beautiful, and he seized the opportunity to charm the pants off the young lady. They were laughing and chatting with one each other, unaware of their surroundings. Basically, everyone was looking at them, wondering what they were saying to each other. Everyone there, in their hearts, could see a connection between the two.

Dinner was amazing, as always, and during and after dinner the men talked politics, and the women talked about anything other than politics. Persian men and their talk of politics drive their women crazy, but that is something the women have to tolerate, since there is not a Persian man out there who doesn't talk about politics. Every Persian man has a solution to Iran's troubles and who should be the savior. Unfortunately, they all differ from one another, so there is very little unity as to who should lead Iran and what the political atmosphere should be in order to ultimately rid Iran of tyranny.

Bandar and his family left around one in the morning and started the long drive home. On the way Bandar started asking questions of his son regarding Henni.

"So, my son, khoob garm gerefte boodi ba dokhtare." (He noted that his son was really sweet-talking the girl). "What were you guys talking about?" Bandar asked with a smile.

"I knew you were going to ask me this," Bandar's son replied after letting out a big laugh responding to his dad's comment.

"I knew you couldn't wait till we were out so you could ask me about her. I know you, Dad. Well, the moment of truth! She is very nice and, as you saw, she is ever so pretty. To be honest, I really like her. Her smarts are equally attractive. She knows so much about everything, Dad. Some of the things she was telling me were blowing my mind. She has read over five hundred books, and she is only twenty-two."

"Five hundred books? *I* haven't even read this many books! Books about what?"

"About anything and everything, Dad. She knows history, geography, philosophy, geology, and of course architecture, since she is an architect."

"Architect? She is so young. Where did she go to school?" Bandar asked.

"In Germany, Dad. She finished her university in her home country of Deutschland. I am so impressed. I asked her out, and she only gave me her number and asked me to call her and talk some more before going on a date. She is the first girl ever in my life who did not say yes to me when I asked her out. She is different, Dad." Bandar's son spoke with a hint of excitement in his voice.

Bandar did not continue the conversation and just carried on with his driving. But in his heart he was smiling. He had a good feeling about this girl and his son. Could she be the one? During the conversation between Bandar and his son about Henni, Bandar's wife kept quiet, which was extremely unusual. When they got home and were in the privacy of their bedroom, she finally broke her silence.

"Bandar, I am not sure how I feel about our son's comments in the car, and I have to say I am confused about this whole Henni business. She is so wonderful, but at the same time she is an illegitimate child, and you know how that is with our culture. On the other hand, I have never seen our son talk about any girl the way he talked about Henni tonight in the car. And the fact that she turned him down says so much about her. She is a khanoom, and this is what our son needs, a lady. I am so confused, Bandar. I have mixed feelings about Henni. Please help me out here."

"My love, why are you confused? If they fall in love and want to be together, then that is a blessing; and to be honest with you, I will be very happy if it does happen. Our son is a good man, but we both know he is a player and no woman has succeeded in winning his heart. He is like a butterfly; he goes from flower to flower. Unfortunately, butterflies don't have a long life. He is young and good-looking now, but we all know it will not last; his butterfly days will be over soon. And for her being an illegitimate child—please, come on! What do you mean by that? We know her father, and her mother is in Germany, so she is not illegitimate. I was very impressed with her. She is such a lady. Very proper, so beautiful with a lovely personality! You heard our son. She is smart also, and that is a quality our son finds attractive. I will ask my dear Buddha to make their union a reality." Bandar kissed his wife on the cheek and embraced her until she fell asleep. This was their routine every night. Bandar hugged his wife and held her and kissed her until she fell asleep, and only then did he close his eyes and go to sleep. Their love and respect for each other was larger than their lives combined and it grew larger everyday.

Bandar's son, after numerous long talks on the phone, succeeded in taking Henni out on a date. A movie date. (My dear readers, please choose a movie.) After their first movie date, they continued seeing each other on a more regular basis. It started with once a week, and after a month it increased to twice a week. After four months of dating without even a single kiss exchanged between them, they finally kissed in a romantic setting on a park bench. The kiss was magical for both of them. They had waited so long for the right moment to kiss, and the park bench on a cool spring night seemed to be as right place as they would ever get. There was no one around. The only sound was the resonance of leaves shaking in the gentle breeze. It was so peaceful. Kissing Henni was one of the most beautiful kisses Bandar's son had ever experienced, and he had kissed many women. It was a kiss with love. True love!

Bandar's son completely changed his ways after that magical kiss. He was finally in love and was experiencing all the feelings that go with being in love. Being in love with Henni felt great. He had never felt like this toward any other woman. Everyone who knew him noticed the change in his mood and attitude. Finally, his lust for more and more women was subdued by the love of a woman. One woman, Ms. Henni Ahmadi. Before the kiss, he still charmed the women when in their company but didn't take it any further than that. After that fateful kiss, he completely stopped flirting with other women. Bandar and his wife were so happy to see their son finally committing to one woman, and not just any woman. It wasn't long before meeting Henni that Bandar's wife asked her son why he could not find a good woman among all the women he knew, and his answer was, "Mom, I haven't found a bad one yet. They are all good." But now he and his family knew he had finally found the true right person in Henni.

Bandar's son proposed to Henni in Stanley Park. He had an engagement ring made for her by a jeweler friend. It was a tapered half-carat diamond ring with two .20-carat sapphire stones on each side of the diamond in an 18-karat white gold band.

He picked Henni up in his new Porsche and took her to their favorite place, Stanley Park. Their routine at the park was to walk together the entire length of the Seawall, talk, hold hands, sit on their favorite park bench and kiss. At Third Beach, Bandar's son suddenly ran off the seawall onto the beach while Henni looked on in surprise. He went to the middle of the beach and in his loudest voice shouted out to Henni, "Ms. Henni Ahmadi, will you marry me?"

He took out the ring from his shorts pocket and held it up while going down on one knee. Whoever was on that particular spot on the beach and the seawall heard Bandar's son's marriage proposal, and now all eyes were on Henni. Henni was looking around, astounded by what just happened, and noticed so many eyes were on her, waiting for her answer. She ran over to Bandar's son on the beach and whispered in his ear. Bandar shouted out, "She said yes!" The whole crowd gave a huge cheer and came over to congratulate the lovely couple. Henni showed off her beautiful ring to everyone, and people were truly in awe with the ring's workmanship and how it glittered.

The couple spent the rest of the day on the beach embracing and kissing, covered in sand. After they watched the sunset together, they first went to Ahmadi's home to announce their engagement, and then Bandar's son drove Henni all the way to his parents' home to announce their engagement to his family. The next day the families got together for lunch to congratulate one another on this wonderful union. Bandar and Ahmadi embraced and cried in each other's arms. Who would have thought a year ago that something like this was going to happen? Last year Ahmadi did not even know he had a daughter. Now, not only did he have a daughter, he also was going to have a son-in-law. Life was beautiful.

Bandar's son and Henni were married in a small ceremony at Bandar's home. There were over sixty guests, and the ceremony was held outdoors on Bandar's estate. Catering was done by a local Persian restaurant, and there was a live band consisting of the groom's friends. They played Persian and Western music, and everyone danced till dawn. At dawn the bride and groom boarded a plane to Germany. A month before the wedding, Henni's mom was diagnosed with cancer, and she was not able to travel for her daughter's wedding, so the newlyweds, instead of going somewhere exotic for their honeymoon, chose to go to Essen to look after Hedda. They were with Hedda for three months, until she succumbed to her cancer and passed away. The doctors had given her two to three weeks, but after seeing Henni with her handsome husband, she lasted much longer than that. After the funeral, Henni and her husband went to the south of Spain for their past-due honeymoon and celebrating Hedda's life in their own terms. Little Homa was conceived in Malaga.

Little Homa was adorable from day one. A newborn who smiled way more than she cried. The parents could not believe how well behaved their little girl was. She slept from nine p.m. till six a.m. straight, without any fuss. At the tender age of two months, she no longer woke up with a cry. She actually woke everyone up with her lovely voice making sounds and laughing. She only cried when she was in some sort of pain. If she was hungry or needed changing, she would baby talk and talk and talk until someone came to her rescue. No one in the family could believe this phenomenon of Little Homa. Bandar's wife even suggested telling her doctor about this, to see if there was anything wrong with Little Homa, since this was so unusual. The doctor's reply: go and count your blessings, you guys are very lucky, there is nothing wrong with her.

Little Homa started walking after her first birthday and talking after sixteen months. She was very good with words and surprised everyone with what she knew through her vocabulary skills. Little Homa loved to talk. She talked to everyone.

Her social skills were phenomenal, and she basked in that glory. Whenever they took her out to restaurants, she would walk around the place and say hello to everyone. Sometimes she even sat on other tables and chatted away with total strangers, having a good laugh, always under the watchful eyes of her mom and dad. She was so cute and friendly that people could not resist her charm. She was as charming as her father and as beautiful as her mother, a killer combination.

Little Homa loved her parents very much, but she longed to be with her grandparents, in particular her grandfathers. She found them very funny and entertaining. She could not understand most of their speech, since for the most part they spoke in Farsi. But the way they talked was animated and funny. She would sit there and observe them for hours. After a while, she knew what they were saying to each other. She had their body language down to a science. She knew when they were sad, when they were happy, when they were arguing, when they were agreeing, when they were tired and sick, when they were passionate, and, the best of them all, when they were hungry. She had completely figured out her grandfathers by age four. However, the grandfathers had not figured her out, because there was really no need for two grown men to figure out their granddaughter. Or was there?

They played with little Homa whenever they got tired of talking to each other. They showered Homa with gifts whenever they saw her, but that was not what Homa wanted. She now wanted to spend more time talking to them than listening, but the grandpas didn't want that. Neither one of them spent much quality time with little Homa until today, the day they are lost under my window.

Today, Homa impresses her grandfathers by showing them a storybook she has done based on the stories she had heard from them. It is a book with illustrated cartoon characters based on her grandfather's stories.

When Bandar, Ahmadi, and little Homa find a coffee shop they can sit in, little Homa takes out a folder from her backpack and hands the folder to her grandfathers. Inside it are a hundred pages of loose paper with illustrations and writings. The illustrations of themselves and the immediate family are astonishing. But what surprises them the most are the illustrations of the people they have described in their stories and conversations. The political figures, the friends, the associates they have mentioned have been drawn with astonishing similarity to their actual features. Bandar and Ahmadi cannot stop looking at the pages of illustrations and writings by their little granddaughter.

"Our granddaughter is a genius, Bandar," Ahmadi tells Bandar while flipping pages.

"Yes, she is a genius, Ahmadi. I am sure she has taken this from my side of the family," Bandar replies jokingly examining her granddaughter's talent.

"Yes right. Oonam to [especially from you]," Ahmadi says with a smile and a wink.

"Have you showed this to anyone, my dear?" Bandar asks little Homa

"No. I have been wanting to show you guys this for a while now but never got the chance. I didn't want to show anyone else except you guys. Do you like it? I did all the artwork myself," she replies excitedly. She has been trying to tell them about this book since she started doing it, but they never gave her the chance. There was always I don't have time or let's play a game or let's go to the park or I need to nap or other excuses that blocked her. This time it was different. They were not talking to each other, and she had their full attention.

"Do we like it? Do we like it she asks," Bandar says while looking at Ahmadi. "We love it, my dear. This is brilliant. You are a genius. Just know you got this from my side of the family."

"Oh, Granddad. You made me so happy. Oh my God, Granddaddy, I love you two so much. Mommy told me that Granddad Ahmadi's family were artists, yes?" Homa replies.

Ahmadi has been silent to this minute, just smiling and admiring his granddaughter. "Yes, my dear. My family goes back generations as artists, so the artist in you comes from our side. But your ingenuity and smarts come from your Granddaddy Bandar's side. You have the best of both worlds, my dear. I love your work, and I think we should talk to your parents about this." Ahmadi gives Homa a big hug and kisses on her cheek.

That night when they bring Homa home, they talk to her parents about what happened that day. They show Henni and her husband the hundred pages of illustrations and writings done by little Homa. Her parents cannot believe their eyes. No way. Homa did all this? How, when, where? So many questions.

"Why do you need to know all these details, my dear ones? Let it be. Accept that your daughter is a genius, and move on. If you pressure her with all these questions, she will freak out and may think she has done something wrong," Ahmadi quietly tells his daughter and son-in-law.

"Ahmadi is right. Let her be. What you need to do is to proofread what she has written and send it to a publisher. First tell her your plans, and see if she wants to have this published. But from what I have read and seen, it will be a shame for it not to get published," Bandar adds.

Both parents stay up and read the entire contents of the folder and look at every single picture. They are impressed. There were many grammatical and spelling errors, but Homa is only six in grade two. However, the content was rich, precise, and funny. The illustrations were vivid and sharp. After finishing reading the book, they make love and sleep. They had one of their best sleeps ever that night.

The following day, little Homa is having breakfast when her parents bring up the storybook. She tells them she really enjoys listening to her grandfathers' stories and based on what she understood she wrote those stories. She basically narrated her grandfathers' funny stories. Homa's parents ask her what she thinks of her book being published.

"What means published?" Homa asks.

"Oh, published is when your book can be read by many other people and they can also enjoy what you have created," her mother replies.

"Okay, if you like it and granddaddies like it, then publish it," Homa says. She starts humming a song, alternating it with eating her cereal.

Homa's book is published a year after the day she showed her granddaddies her work. The family chooses to self publish, and her book becomes popular with both young and old readers, Persians and non-Persians. The book was written in English, but every Persian can relate to her stories. Success is upon the family through little Homa. "We have many more stories for you, my dear. You want to go for a bike ride?" Bandar asks little Homa

"Sure, let's go. Where is Granddad Ahmadi?" Homa asks in return.

"He said to call him and let him know what we are doing, and he will join us. Where do you want to go riding, dear?" Bandar grabs Homa's small hand in his and walks toward his car.

"Stanley Park, Granddad. Let's go to Stanley Park," Homa replies.

(My dear readers, again it's your turn to contribute. Who do you think in this story made the sacrifices through love to become content?)

CPSIA information can be obtained
at www.ICGtesting.com
Printed in the USA
BVHW030551210921
617105BV00003B/4